HOPE SPARKS

HARLEY TATE

HOPE SPARKS

A POST-APOCALYPTIC SURVIVAL THRILLER

Six weeks into the apocalypse, would you have hope?

From an emergency landing, to a full-blown riot, to a militia gone rogue, Colt and Walter have survived it all. Joining forces, their group heads toward Walter's cabin and the promise of a new life. But mother nature has other plans.

When your life is in danger, can you summon the courage to fight?

Madison and Tracy think they're safe at a cabin in woods. But a chance meeting with a stranger reveals how vulnerable they really are. Faced with an unpredictable threat, the pair must defend their new home, even when the odds are stacked against them.

The end of the world brings out the best and worst in all of us.

Dangerous wild animals, hidden traps on the road, and violent strangers combine to push everyone to the limit. If Walter and Colt can't make it back home in time, Madison and Tracy might not survive. It's a battle against nature and man that only the strong will survive.

The EMP is only the beginning.

Hope Sparks is book seven in the *After the EMP* series, a post-apocalyptic thriller series following ordinary people trying to survive after a geomagnetic storm destroys the nation's power grid.

* * *

Subscribe to Harley's newsletter and receive an exclusive companion short story, *Darkness Falls*, absolutely free.
www.harleytate.com/subscribe

* * *

PROLOGUE

COLT

Northern California Forest
  6:30 a.m.

Colt's breath steamed into the cool foothill air as he eased into a crouch on the water's edge. The marshes around the edge of the pond held more ducks than a man could eat in a lifetime. Lottie sat beside him, alert and waiting.

The first hint of a call sounded in the distance and Colt readied his shotgun. A single V of five birds swooped low and circled. Colt waited. As they came in for a soft landing, Colt fired. One fell into the water and Lottie took off like a miniature torpedo.

The rest of the flock scrambled into the air, squawking and carrying on. Colt stood up. Five minutes later, a soaked little Lottie came swimming back with a bird twice her size in her teeth. Never in his life did he think a five-pound dog bred to fit in a purse would turn into a ferocious little hunter. But Lottie loved to retrieve.

She dropped the duck at his feet and shook her whole body from nose to tail. Water droplets flew everywhere and Colt fished a piece of jerky from his pocket. He fed it to the little dog, patted her head, and picked up the duck. By the time they made it back to camp, everyone else was awake and starting the day.

Dani crouched in front of the fire, getting it going just how Walter taught her. Larkin stood at the smoker, tending to the deer he'd killed the day before. Walter rummaged through their growing supply of dried plants and roots.

All together, they made an efficient four-person team. It wouldn't be long before Walter amassed everything he needed and then some. Colt hoped when the time came, Walter would decide to bring them all along.

He set the duck down on the prep table they had fashioned out of cut branches and walked over to Dani. The wound on her cheek was healing well, and thanks to Walter's even stitches, it might not leave too jagged a scar. Every day that went by away from Eugene and without conflict, Dani brightened. Gone were the pensive stares and somber moments when Colt wondered if she would ever laugh again.

If they could find some stability in this ever-changing world, she had the potential to grow into an amazing adult. Colt crouched beside her. "So what's on the menu today?"

She smiled. "Miner's lettuce, chicory root coffee, and guess what else?" Her eyes glittered as she waited.

"Deer jerky?"

"Nope."

"Duck meat."

"Try again."

"Smoked trout."

Dani laughed. "Eggs! Walter found a nest of quail eggs!"

"Don't get too excited." Walter's voice carried across the camp. "They're small and we only have four."

Colt grinned. "Now if we could just make some sausage, we'd be set."

"It's on the list. Find me some cloves and cayenne pepper and we're in business."

The tidy camp lapsed into silence as everyone went back to work. In no time, they'd put together a breakfast most people would have paid a premium for only a few weeks ago.

Colt eased to the ground beside Dani and watched as Walter tinkered with the radio. Thanks to the Humvee's battery and netting poles, they were able to not only receive radio frequencies, but broadcast as well.

Walter cleared his throat, moved a few knobs and began his morning broadcast. "Good morning. The time is 7:30 Pacific Standard, and it has been thirty-nine days since the United States power grid failed. My name is Walter Sloane."

He glanced over at Dani and smiled. "If this is your first time listening to my broadcasts, welcome. We have been through some of the most trying times we've ever had to face as a country. But we will persevere. If you are out there listening this morning, that means you are a survivor. You have found a way to keep going when the odds were stacked against you. Don't give up now. Together, we can weather this storm."

Dani leaned against Colt as Walter kept talking, describing the things people could do to find water or food. He couldn't help but wonder what Walter's own family was doing now. Were they listening to him? Did they know he was safe? Sooner or later, Walter would head home, and the three of them—Colt, Dani, and Larkin—would need to find their own way.

But for now, they were safe in the woods. With shelters made from Douglas fir and beds of matted pine straw, they were comfortable at night. Daily hunting and gathering provided enough to eat. The nearby creek gave them all the water they could ask for. It wasn't a home in a good neighborhood with a manicured lawn and a new car in the driveway.

It was better.

Walter continued and Colt sat back to listen. "Over the past week, I've learned that family isn't what's written on your birth certificate or determined by your last name. It's about finding like-minded people to share life's burdens. People you can trust. Yes, we're faced with challenging times, but don't let adversity stop you. Find others who want to survive and band together.

"You might not have much, but you're still breathing. You're still alive. So take in that next breath with hope and courage and optimism. This isn't the end of our country or our way of life. This isn't the end of you. It's a new beginning. Grab it with both hands and never let go."

Walter glanced at Colt before continuing. "I might not be broadcasting for a while after today, but don't worry. I'll be back before you know it. Until next time, this is Walter Sloane. Good luck." He clicked off the radio and exhaled.

Something in Walter's words and glance said what Colt suspected. He eased away from Dani as he called out to his new friend. "So this is it?"

Walter nodded. "It's time. Thanks to all of you, I have more than I need and way more than I can transport."

Dani shifted on the ground, her face scrunched up in question. "What's going on?"

Larkin picked at a pinecone. "Walter's packing up. He's going home."

"But…what about the camp and all the work we've put into it?"

Colt managed a sad smile. "We still get to use it."

Dani's gaze shifted from Colt to Walter as understanding spread across her face. "We aren't leaving."

"About that." Walter stood up and brushed off the dirt clinging to his pants. "What would you say about coming with me?"

"To your home?"

"It's not mine exactly. It belongs to another family. I don't know if they will accept you."

"But you're willing to bring us along?"

Dani reached for Colt's arm. "I don't want to cause anyone else problems."

Walter held up a hand. "When we arrive, we'll explain the situation and put it up to a vote. If it doesn't work, you can go on your way or come back here."

Colt glanced at Dani. He thought about all she still needed to learn. All she would miss tagging along with two grown military men in the woods. "Are there kids Dani's age?"

"College kids. Four or five years older."

Better than nothing. He reached out and squeezed her hand. "We'll come. And if it doesn't work out, no hard feelings."

Walter smiled. "Good. Because there's no way I can get there on my own."

SIX WEEKS WITHOUT POWER

DAY FORTY-THREE

CHAPTER ONE

MADISON

Clifton Compound
8:00 a.m.

The soft earth crumbed beneath the weight of the spade as Madison dug a shallow trough. Before the grid failed, she spent every day planting, watering, and checking on the health of her plants. But at night she went home to a lit-up dorm room, dining hall, and trusty laptop.

These days the only welcome was a small cot and a warm spot left by a little orange cat. The EMP changed everything. Without power, the cities devolved into chaos. Mass looting and riots. Panic and lawlessness. Her father barely escaped downtown Sacramento alive.

The creeps calling Chico State home almost took them all out. If it weren't for her father and her college roommate, Madison would be dead. She leaned back on her heels and stared at the ground.

No more movie nights or all-night study sessions beneath the glow of a desk lamp. No more cell phones or computers or modern tech. They were back to square one: seeds, dirt, and prayers for rain. Agrarian skills were the new finance degree, sustainable crops the new hedge fund.

"Didn't know staring at a garden would help the plants grow."

Madison glanced up. Her former college roommate and now closest friend stood in front of her, rifle resting on her forearm like it belonged there since birth. "Finished your rounds?"

Brianna nodded. "Nothing to see except a scrawny squirrel and a teenage farm girl who bit off more than she can chew."

Madison raised an eyebrow. "What are you talking about?"

"This plot of land. It's enormous. You really think you can plant and maintain it all?"

Madison stared out at the twenty rows of earth. Their survival depended on a healthy garden yield. With seven mouths to feed, they needed every tomato, carrot, pea, and head of lettuce they could harvest. Asparagus and broccoli would help, too.

If she had her wish, she would have three gardens this size, an expanded orchard, and trained wild blackberries in the forest. As long as she stayed at the Cliftons' place, Madison would contribute. The more the better.

The alternative wasn't something she wanted to consider. Failure would mean wasted seeds, empty plates, and hardship in the summer. Starvation in the winter. Even if her father managed to kill every deer in the surrounding forest, they would need more than venison jerky to ride out the snowy months ahead.

Madison leaned back on her heels. "I can do it. It won't be easy, but the soil is already tilled thanks to Peyton's hard work. The rain the past few days has softened it. Once we rig up some rain barrels, it'll almost take care of itself."

"What about the animals that will root through the crops? I've seen a ton of squirrels and birds. Won't they cause problems?"

"We can solve that with some scarecrows and netting."

Brianna adjusted the bandana barely holding back her curls with a frown. "What about intruders? If anyone comes across this place in the summer, they could clear it out before we even know they're here."

Madison snorted in frustration. Brianna held valid concerns, but what was the alternative? "Would you rather starve or use up all your parents' supplies?"

"Of course not."

"Then we don't have a choice. We need this size garden and we need to protect it." Madison pointed at the tree line. "We can string up a trip wire around the entire place with cans and cover it up with branches and leaves. As soon as someone runs into it, we'll hear them. It won't keep a person out, but we'll know if someone finds the garden."

Brianna squinted into the sun. "I wish we had a watchdog. That would solve a lot of problems."

"Fireball can't fend off a thief, but he'll help with the critters."

"He'll get fat if he keeps catching as many mice as he's managed lately."

Madison smiled. The little cat loved the property and the surrounding forest. He hunted all night and sprawled out in a little patch of sun on the porch all day. It was cat paradise. Thanks to the generosity of Brianna and her family, not only Fireball, but Madison, her mom, dad, and friend Peyton all had a home. It was a place they could do more than survive the day. It was somewhere they could live.

Breathe. Sleep at night.

When the grid failed, Brianna helped them leave school and hit the road. She was the reason Madison and Peyton were alive. Madison owed her former roommate and her parents this garden. It would have to work.

Madison picked up the box of seeds beside her. "You ever think about what everyone from school is doing now?"

"No."

Madison blinked. "Not once?"

"Never." Brianna turned away, hiding her face from view. Her voice carried over her shoulder. "What's the point? They're either dead or will be."

"I guess I—" Madison faltered, unsure what to say. Brianna's boyfriend Tucker died on the way to the cabin.

After his makeshift funeral, Brianna acted as if college never existed. If Madison or Peyton brought up UC Davis, Brianna shut down or checked out.

She channeled all of her hurt and sadness into scouting missions or chopping firewood or inventorying their supplies. Brianna didn't stop working until she collapsed into bed at night. It made for productive days, but Madison worried about what was going on inside her head. Did she think about Tucker? Did she blame herself for his death?

Madison would never be able to repay Brianna for the kindness of bringing her family to safety, but she wished she could ease the twenty-year-old's burden. She stood up with the box of seeds under her arm. "I'm about to plant two rows of peas. Would you like to help?"

Brianna turned back around, her eyes glassy and bright. "I need to check on the traps."

The mention of hunting roiled Madison's stomach. Her father was out in the forest, miles and miles away from the cabin, hunting and gathering as much food as he could. Walter Sloane wasn't a man for sitting around or failing to contribute. After only two days at the cabin, Madison's father packed up and headed north. No one knew when he was coming home.

"Your dad will be all right. He's tough as nails."

Madison scrunched her nose. "Is it obvious?"

"That you're worried?" Brianna flashed a weak smile. "Yeah, but your secret's safe with me." Stretching her arms wide, she closed her eyes and tilted her head toward the sun. As she relaxed, she slung her rifle onto her shoulder. "I guess hunting can wait. Let's plant some peas."

"Are you sure? I can manage if you need to go."

Brianna shrugged. "Some company could do me good. Besides, it's about time I learned some of this stuff."

Together the two young women planted the rows, with Madison explaining depth of seed and ratio of soil to water. By the time they finished, a dusting of dirt covered their jeans and sweat dampened their backs.

"This is hard work."

"Wait until the harvest comes in. We'll be picking all day."

Brianna stared down the mounded row of earth they made. "What will we do with all the produce?"

"Cook, can, dehydrate. You name it. If there's a way to preserve it, we have to try. I do *not* want to end up like the Donner party."

"Ew. I don't care how hungry I am, eating dead people is not on my list of acceptable options."

"Even if you're starving?"

Brianna shook her head. "Not a chance. If I'm resorting to cannibalism, then I'm finding a fresh one."

Madison groaned. "You're so gross."

"Is she making you smell her stinky armpits again?" Peyton bounded into the clearing and stopped a few steps away. At over six feet and built like a football player, he practically blotted out the morning sun.

"We were discussing the finer points of cannibalism, if you must know."

Peyton pulled a face. "Please tell me you're joking."

Brianna reached up and squeezed his arm, pretending to test it for muscle. "Afraid we'll eat you first?"

Peyton pointed at his thighs. "There's no oven big enough for these legs. But Madison over there is just the right size for that stock pot your mom uses to heat water."

"Am not!"

"Are too!"

The three former college kids erupted into a fit of laughter. After a moment, Madison wiped at her eyes. "At least the end of the world hasn't killed our sense of humor."

"Never." Peyton leaned over and wrapped Madison in a sideways hug. "Want something else to cheer you up?"

She eyed him with suspicion. "Don't tell me you've tried to cook breakfast again."

"Not a chance. But I did figure out how to power the radio."

Madison swallowed. "You did?"

"I haven't heard anyone broadcasting yet, but there's always a chance. It's set up on the main porch."

Madison scooped up her supplies and headed straight toward the line of trees and the kitchen cabin. If her father could find a way to broadcast, he would. She wanted to be there to hear it.

CHAPTER TWO

WALTER

Northern California Forest
11:10 a.m.

WALTER KNEELED IN FRONT OF THE RADIO AND WATCHED the faces of two people he had come to count on as more than friends. Dani scowled at the dirt. Colt's brow wrinkled and his teeth clenched. Although Colt volunteered to make the journey with Walter back to the Cliftons' cabin, a few days' delay let doubts creep in.

Thanks to steady drizzle and a terrain impossible to navigate without traction or the sun, Walter had been forced to put his departure on hold. But the sun shone this morning and the ground was dry enough to drag supplies along without digging a trench a mile deep. It was time to go.

He began to pack the radio. It had been a long two weeks in the woods of Northern California and

Walter was thankful for the daily radio talks. He didn't know if anyone heard his voice as he spoke into the void, but it centered him and gave him focus.

He glanced at Colt as the man crouched down beside him. "Did I sound all right this morning?"

Colt nodded.

"Thank you again for the radio. I'd missed broadcasting." Five days of steady on-time broadcasts and calm had seeped back into Walter's bones.

"Glad to help. I heard you one night in Eugene and thought you might want to pick it back up."

Walter blinked. Colt heard him all the way up in Oregon?

They first met the day the power grid failed: an airline pilot and an air marshal. Chance put them on the same plane, but a solar storm destroyed the grid while they watched from 37,000 feet in the air. Walter landed the plane on a private runway and Colt kept order in the passenger cabin, but they parted ways the day after the EMP.

Thanks to a strange coincidence, and maybe some luck, they were back together again. Walter eased onto his heels as he thought about all that transpired in between. Making it down to Sacramento, barely escaping riots with his life, finding his family, and trekking to Truckee.

He asked Colt a question he'd often wondered. "Did it make a difference?"

"The broadcast?" Colt scratched his beard. "It did to me. Gave me hope. I knew you'd gone to

Sacramento. If you were still alive, that meant all of us in Eugene had a chance to make it, too."

"Good." Walter let a smile show. "All I want is to give people the strength to carry on. If I can reach even one person…"

"Then you'll have done something."

Walter nodded. "Thank you."

"Anytime." Colt stood and made his way across the little camp in the woods to where a teenage girl sat with a scrap of a dog in her lap. Dani might not be related to Colt by blood, but the two were as close as Walter and his daughter Madison.

Walter thought about all the displaced families. All the people who were stuck like he was, hundreds or thousands of miles away from home, when the EMP hit. Madison had been so damn lucky.

If she'd gone on spring break like so many of her friends, would she be alive today? How would any college kid make it home from a beach in Mexico or a ski trip in the mountains?

At any moment in America, millions of people were flying, driving, riding on buses or trains. All going somewhere. When the EMP hit, how many were hundreds or thousands of miles away?

Six weeks later, how many were still alive? How many who struggled today would survive the winter?

Walter wasn't sure the Clifton family would accept Colt, Dani, or their friend, James Larkin, but he had to try. Leaving them out in the forest with no shelter wasn't an option.

His knees cracked and popped as he stood. Making

his way across the camp, Walter paused in front of Colt and Dani. Their little dog, Lottie, yipped at him and Walter bent to scratch her head. "It's time for me to go. The ground is dry enough and I need to seize the opportunity."

Dani nodded, but didn't say a word.

"Like I said before, I was hoping you would come with me."

Dani glanced up, her lower lip caught between her teeth.

Walter pressed on. "I don't know if the owners will let you stay, but I owe you a debt of gratitude. Not only did I welcome the company, but you made short work of all my tasks."

Colt rose up, rubbing his face as he looked around the camp. "I know I agreed before, but I've got some doubts. I'm not sure we should impose."

"Like I said, there's no guarantee you can stay."

Dani dug a trench in the dirt with her shoe, bending forward until stringy brown hair covered her face. She didn't say a word. Not the warm reception Walter had hoped for. Lottie, the little dog belonging to one of their former group members, crouched against her feet, trembling.

Despite weighing only a handful of pounds, the little Yorkie proved herself a fearsome watchdog and retriever. Too bad her owner didn't have the same will to survive. Melody was one of many to die in the last few weeks.

From what Colt explained, most of their group perished in one grisly way or another. If it wasn't at the hands of a rogue militia, then nature or anger or fear swallowed them up, one by one.

Walter knew the dangers the current state of the country would bring. While the three people sharing his camp would be helpful as time wore on, their stockpile of guns and ammo could be invaluable. He wanted them to come with him, not just for the company, but for the protection they could provide.

A former Navy SEAL, Army major, and a scrappy teenager who fought off more men in the last forty-five days than MMA fighters over the course of a career. They were a motley, well-seasoned crew. Walter and the rest of his group could use their wits and muscle.

Convincing everyone to take a chance would be a challenge.

The lean-to constructed at the edge of the camp rustled to life. Major James Larkin's sandy-blond head emerged from the pine boughs and drying leaves. He paused after stretching to his full height.

"Whoa. Somebody else die or what?" He made a show of counting the group on his fingers. "All remaining members present and accounted for, so what the hell is wrong?"

Walter spoke up. "It's time I head back."

Larkin's lips thinned for a moment before he recovered. "I see." His attention turned to Colt. "I suppose we should be on our way, then."

Colt didn't move from Dani's side. "Walter's offer still stands. He wants us to come with him."

"For what, protection?"

"Or to stay." Colt let out a breath and glanced at Walter. "We could make a trade: weapons for lodging."

Walter kept the shock off his face. That Colt would be willing to give up some of their haul in exchange for a place to stay showed the good in him. Walter needed them to come.

Dani disagreed. "Colt, no!" She scooped up Lottie and jumped to her feet. "Look what happened last time we stayed with someone." She clutched the only living member of the group Colt and Dani befriended in Eugene to her chest. The dog yipped.

"The kid's got a point." Larkin ran a hand through his hair before letting out a low whistle. "Death seems to follow us around."

"I don't believe that." Walter walked over to the wood pile and picked up two more logs. He added them to the dwindling fire as he spoke. "Colt explained what happened. Those people made their own choices. You didn't kill them."

"Might as well have." Dani stroked the dog's fur as she looked to Colt for support. "We can't go."

Colt stared at her for a moment before glancing at Larkin. "There's no harm in checking it out. We have to go somewhere; we can't stay in the forest forever."

Walter seized the opportunity to push his point. "We could use a few more hands at the cabin. Combine your skills with the weapon stash you're lugging around and I'm sure the owners will see the value in your addition to the group."

Larkin pressed on with Dani's concerns. "We don't have the best track record of keeping people alive."

Walter shook his head. "You won't need to protect us. We're hardened to the reality of this new life." He jabbed the logs with a poker made out of hardwood. "Not to say we won't appreciate the support, because we would. But we're not helpless. You won't shoulder the entire burden. You'll share it."

Larkin focused on the flames as they licked the new logs. At last, he conceded. "If Colt's in, I'm in. Even if your group doesn't welcome us to stay, the least we can do is get you there safe and sound." He nodded as he spoke, solidifying the decision. "We can leave as easily as we come."

Walter turned to Colt. "What about you?"

"Say no, Colt." Dani's voice warbled as she protested. "We can't risk it."

Colt glanced at Dani, his jaw set and tense. "We could have a place to stay, Dani. A home. Kids closer to your age."

She snorted. "Look how well that turned out last time."

The man winced, but he turned to Walter. "It wouldn't be fair to send you on your way with all this gear. The least we can do is help you get home."

Walter nodded. "Thank you. Like I said, no promises. But once the rest of the group meets you, I can't imagine them sending you away." He turned to Dani. "We won't force you to stay. If you want to leave after you meet everyone, that's okay. But you could use a few days of rest."

Larkin let out a short chuckle. "Is that what you do there, rest?"

Walter shook his head with a smile. "No. I don't think anyone will be resting for very long now. Not if they want to survive."

Larkin clapped his hands. "Then what are we waiting for? Let's get packing."

CHAPTER THREE

COLT

Northern California Forest
3:00 p.m.

"We can't go with Walter." Dani walked beside Colt while they made a final circle of the camp. Leaves and twigs crunched beneath their feet. "Everyone we get to know dies. I can't go through that again. I can't get another family killed."

Lottie scampered ahead of them, snuffling out an animal's tracks in the underbrush. Colt focused on the little dog who'd proved herself more valuable than many of the people he'd met over the past six weeks. She might be happy camping out in makeshift shelter in the woods now with moderate daytime temperatures and lows in the fifties, but come winter, even Lottie would want a permanent home.

"We have to think ahead, Dani. The winter in this

area will be brutal. There could be a foot of snow on the ground, maybe more. We need to prepare now. Come November, living in the forest won't be an option."

"Then we find an abandoned place and take it over. We don't need anyone else."

As they approached the first of ten snares set up in a circle around the camp, Colt brought his finger to his lips. He slowed, hoping an unsuspecting rabbit took the bait, but no such luck. The snare sat empty and loose.

He dismantled the wire while Lottie gobbled up the blob of peanut butter left as bait. "You can't ignore what Walter's done for us. Thanks to him we had a chance to heal, gather food, and stay warm at night. We've slept, Dani. Actually slept more than a handful of minutes a night. Do you know how valuable that is?"

She chewed on her lip while Colt worked, staring at his hands but not really seeing them. The girl had been through so much, but still she fought to stay alive. Colt wished he could give her a safe home, a warm bed, and all the food they could ever need.

But he couldn't promise a miracle. Walter was the key to that.

As he stood up and stowed the snare supplies, Dani sighed. "Fine. We can get him home. But we aren't staying."

Colt kept a smile to himself. Getting her there was the hard part. If the compound was anything close to what Walter described, Dani would want to stay. "Let's take down the rest of the snares as quick as we can. We need to help Walter and Larkin pack."

"How are we going to carry everything? Walter's

assembled way more than we can manage. Even if we made some sort of a sled it wouldn't be enough."

This time, Colt didn't hold back. A smile cracked his dry lips. "Larkin's got that under control."

Dani's eyebrows pinched, but she said nothing, opting instead to check the next snare. They lapsed into silence as they worked, each one veering off the main circular route to check the traps.

All the snares sat empty and unsprung. Either the animals in the forest wised up to their methods, or they had cleared the immediate vicinity of most easy-to-trap critters.

The lack of success solidified Colt's determination. Moving on wasn't just an option; it was a necessity. He entered the camp with Dani and Lottie by his side and nothing to show for their efforts.

Walter glanced up from a crouch. His gaze flitted over their empty hands and grim faces. "No luck?"

"Not today."

He nodded. "Something's spooked the animals."

"Another storm?"

"Maybe. But it's time to go. We should get moving."

Colt set to work dismantling the shelter he'd shared with Dani since they arrived. Constructed of full pine branches crisscrossed on top of stripped saplings, they had been dry even with rainy, damp nights. The bedding of loose pine needles left a bit to be desired, but thanks to extra clothes recovered from the Humvee and pickup, they managed to stay warm.

Tugging the branches off one by one, Colt dispersed

them throughout the area and kicked dirt and leaves on top to conceal any evidence of their camp. The last thing they needed was a band of desperate people following their tracks to Walter's cabin.

Leaving a camp in good working order would only invite questions and curiosity. Better to destroy it than take the chance.

Dani gathered all their personal gear, shoving sweaters and pants into the backpacks that survived the escape from Eugene and subsequent crash along the rural highway. She worked with quiet efficiency, only stopping now and then to shower Lottie with affection.

After an hour of steady work, no sign of the shelter or their clothes and personal gear remained. Colt turned toward Walter. The man leaned over a small sack of wild ginger roots, pressing the air out before rolling the top down to create a waterproof seal.

"How can we help?"

Walter glanced up. "Can you figure out the best way to dispose of all the cooking supplies? The solar cooker and dehydrator will never make the trip, but we can't leave them here. Same goes for any of our trash we haven't burned."

Colt nodded. "I'll get the shovel."

Five minutes later, the point of the shovel bit into the soft forest floor and Colt scooped up a load of dirt and debris before dumping it off to the side. Everything they couldn't take with them or dispose of another way would have to be buried. Judging by the pile of items building beside him, Colt would be busy for a while.

Walter carried over a bundle of stripped branches used as skewers for drying meat over the smokehouse. He hesitated before dropping them on the ground. "What if we make two pits? One for things we could come back to retrieve and one for trash?"

Colt nodded. "Already thought of it. This is the keep pit. I'll dig a trash pit on the other side of the clearing."

Walter nodded. "Good. I'll separate the supplies." He crouched beside the assembled items before pulling apart the solar cooker and folding the cardboard and aluminum foil into manageable packets. "Every time I pick up something that rolled off an assembly line, I start thinking. Paper. Two-by-fours. Cardboard. So many things we can't make anymore. How long before we run out of aluminum foil and toilet paper?"

"There have to be massive distribution warehouses full of the stuff."

"Any that haven't been ransacked?"

Colt gave it some thought. "There have to be. Transportation is the problem. People can break in, but how do they move it all? Without working gas stations, most trucks are out of commission at this point."

"We rigged the Humvee up on vegetable oil. Other people probably did that, too."

Colt nodded at Dani. "Yeah, but it only lasted what, two hundred miles? Without the proper filters, oil isn't a long-term solution."

When Colt first walked into Walter's camp, he'd been blown away at the man's ingenuity. Harvesting food from the forest was genius. But the more Colt thought about it, the more he could see the utility in a different sort of gathering mission.

A huge, multi-person operation aimed at distribution centers. "Anyone know where the nearest Walmart distribution warehouse is located?"

Dani stared at him with blank eyes.

Walter rocked his head back and forth, estimating. "Can't be that far from here. I couldn't imagine they'd use expensive real estate, so that leaves Tahoe and Reno out. Truckee might be a good place."

"How far are we?"

Walter glanced up at the sky as he thought. "From downtown? Fifty miles, maybe."

"How many miles between the cabin and downtown?"

"Thirty. It's secluded, but not that remote."

Colt didn't say any more, but a plan percolated in his mind. If he could convince Dani to stay at Walter's place, he knew how he could prove his usefulness without giving up all of their weapons.

It would solidify his willingness to contribute and give them a leg up heading into winter. He thought about the Camaro and the transport driver who T-boned the pickup truck. The man had been a gun runner. That meant a compound with gear, weapons, and food. A militia.

He glanced at Walter. "Tell me about Cunningham again."

Walter shook his head. "I've told you everything I know. The man's a fanatic; some sort of religious zealot who's convinced this is the rapture."

"What about his compound? The people staying with him? Are they close by?"

"I don't know. We've only run into them once and that was enough. We've tried to stay as far away from them as possible. That's why I chose to come out here alone. Easier to evade them that way."

Dani spoke up. "But you invited us to stay. Why would you do that if it put you at risk?"

Walter nodded in agreement. "Because I realized the foolhardy nature of my plan. Sure I could run, but I'd lose all my supplies." He smirked. "It helped that you showed up with duffel bags full of weapons."

"Cunningham's men must be looking for them. They'll want to make a trade."

Walter shook his head. "Don't get any ideas. We are *not* engaging with him. The less they know about us, the better. "

Colt wasn't so sure. A strong enough show of force and maybe they could live side by side as trading partners. If Cunningham's men discovered the cabin, which they would eventually, it might not end as peacefully as Walter hoped. Cutting off the chance for an ambush might be the best approach.

But they could worry about that later. Colt shoved the thoughts to the side. Getting to the cabin and meeting the others was the priority. He couldn't get ahead of himself.

The sound of crunching leaves alerted everyone and Lottie took off like a rocket toward the noise. She reappeared a minute later running circles around

Larkin's feet. The former army major grinned ear to ear.

"Good news?"

Larkin jangled a set of car keys in front of him. "Who wants a ride?"

CHAPTER FOUR

TRACY

"HOW LONG WILL IT TAKE ALL THIS TO TURN INTO compost?"

Anne Clifton hoisted a shovel full of steaming kitchen scraps into the air and scrunched up her nose as she thought it over. "Six months. Maybe a year. Come next spring, we can mix this pile into the garden along with the toilet compost and have an excellent fertilizer."

Tracy blinked. "Toilet compost?"

Anne chuckled as she stabbed the decaying pile again with the shovel. "Haven't you noticed the dry toilet?"

"Of course. But I just assumed it was like an outhouse."

"Nope. It's a composting toilet. All the waste flows to

a collection chamber out the back of the wash house and the solar panels on the roof power the fans inside. We don't have to do anything to it except empty it every few months."

"And what comes out is compost?"

"Some of the best there is."

Tracy stared at Brianna's mother in disbelief. Composting human waste never crossed Tracy's mind. She'd always assumed they would be building a new facility when the pit beneath the toilet filled up. It never occurred to her to look at the back of the building.

She glanced at the cabins now. The Cliftons had built their property in stages: first a small cabin with a kitchen and communal living space, then a wash house, and finally a bunk house. All told, they had room for twelve. More, if some of the communal space was converted back to sleeping areas.

Between the kitchen and the bunkhouse sat a small garden plot used for herbs and flowers. Past the cabins, pasture land stretched for an acre, yielding enough grass to rotate a few pigs and chickens. A small orchard of fruit and nut trees lined the area beyond the pasture and past them, Madison and Peyton planned to start a larger garden.

Ten acres, forest all around, and not a single neighbor for half a mile. Brianna's family found a way to carve out a bit of paradise in the foothills of California and Tracy couldn't be more thankful. She thrust her own shovel into the decaying compost and lifted a scoop into the air. The more movement of the decaying matter, and the more oxygen surrounding the leftover bits of food, the faster the heap would transform into fertilizer.

"Thank you again for welcoming us into your home."

Anne glanced up and her blue eyes shone. She looked every bit her daughter's relation with graying curls and the same fiery spirit. "You're welcome. Like I said before, we can use the hands."

Since the minute Tracy, Walter, and the kids arrived, Anne and Barry Clifton put them to work. Madison and Peyton tilled a plot for a garden on the edge of the property. Brianna helped her dad hunt and set up a perimeter defense. Tracy spent her days helping preserve as much food as possible and keep the homestead in good working order.

With seven mouths to feed and bodies to clothe, no task was easy.

"Meeeoowww." Fireball bumped his head into Tracy's skin before slinking between her legs and winding himself around her calf.

She bent to give the cat a scratch. "At least we don't have an eighth mouth to feed. You're doing quite well keeping the mice away."

Anne smiled. "That he is. A cat was one of the main problems we couldn't solve while building this place. It's not like you can keep a good mouser in a vacuum-sealed bag until you need him. I'm thankful you had the sense to bring your cat along."

Fireball rubbed against Tracy's leg and she gave him one more scratch. "He wasn't ours. I found him at my former boss's apartment complex. She——" Tracy paused as the memories of Wanda's death filled her mind. "She didn't adjust to the grid collapse as well as she could."

"I'm sorry."

Tracy waved Anne off and stood up. "It's okay. I'm sure you lost people, too."

Anne nodded. "Our neighbors in Stockton didn't appreciate the danger. Barry practically begged John to come with us. They refused." Anne frowned as she stared at the still-steaming compost pile. "I'm sure they're dead by now. Mary wouldn't even take a case of water. Kept saying FEMA or the Red Cross would be there soon."

Tracy snorted. "Neither one showed up in our neighborhood."

"I never saw them, either."

"Walter hitched a ride with the National Guard to make it to Sacramento, but they weren't there to hand out supplies."

Anne's lips thinned. "Let me guess. Riot control?"

Tracy nodded. "They barricaded downtown. Wouldn't let anyone in or out. Walter and his copilot barely escaped."

"What happened to the copilot? Did he make it home?"

Tracy swallowed. "He died helping us." This time she couldn't hold back the emotion. A sob slipped past her lips and she covered her mouth with the back of her hand. "So many people have died. And because of what?"

"False sense of security. Lack of self-reliance. No knowledge of history or our place in it." Anne stepped away from the compost and reached for Tracy's shovel. "If we don't remember the past and our struggles in this country, how can we be expected to persevere in the face of hardship?"

"I worry about the future we're creating for the kids. Brianna, Madison, and Peyton. How will they become adults?"

Anne smiled. "Same way we did. One day at a time." She turned toward the cabins and Tracy followed.

Halfway there, a low hiss from Fireball stopped the women cold. Tracy reached for the handgun tucked behind the waist of her jeans and brought it up to her chest. Anne set one shovel down before rising up to hold the other like a battle axe.

Thirty feet separated the women from the main cabin. No cover. Not even a bush or scraggly tree to hide behind. Tracy motioned to the wash house. "Head that way. I'll go to the front."

Anne nodded and took off, shovel still tight in her hands. With her left hand gripped tight on the slide, Tracy racked a round into the chamber with a quick push forward of the grip. It wasn't the way Walter loaded a handgun, but Tracy didn't have the grip strength of a forty-five-year-old man used to handling weapons. Pushing instead of pulling allowed her to use the strength of her chest muscles and not risk jamming a round.

She eased forward with the gun low in front of her and her finger light along the frame. Before the grid failed, she never thought to carry any type of gun, concealed or not. Now she didn't step outside without one.

Creeping up to the cabin's rear corner, Tracy watched Fireball slink ahead. With ears flat, he advanced, his body skimming the ground. Trusting a cat to alert on an intruder seemed crazy, but Tracy couldn't ignore the crest of orange fur standing on end or the way Fireball inched forward.

Someone or something lurked beyond the cabin's front door.

Tracy took a calming breath. The kids were safe on the other side of the property planting another section of the garden before nightfall. Walter was off on his foraging mission. Barry set off earlier in the day for a fishing expedition; they didn't expect him back for two days at least.

They were at their weakest right this moment, but she had fifteen rounds in the magazine of the Glock 19 and she could hit a man's chest dead center. It wasn't how she wanted to end the day. Killing an intruder would be the last resort.

It could be a lost hiker in need of some charity and kindness. A child alone in the woods with nowhere to go. An injured animal falling down due to a broken leg or damaged paw.

Tracy inhaled and exhaled through her mouth. *Steady now.* She eased toward the front corner of the cabin, skirting by the kitchen window. The closer she came to the front, the more Fireball's fur rose. He looked like a caricature of a cat with his back arching in an upside down U and his claws digging into the earth.

No matter the danger, Tracy would face it head on. She stepped to the corner and eased her head forward. *Oh, no.*

Not ten feet in front of her stood a solitary man. No pack on his back. No hunting rifle. A man who would have looked at home on a city street in Sacramento in his skinny jeans and printed T-shirt. His hands were hidden behind his back and he stood in the middle of the gravel drive, staring up at the cabin with half a smile.

Crazy? Hopeful? Certainly not injured. One hundred percent dangerous.

Tracy raised the Glock and stepped clear of the building.

CHAPTER FIVE

TRACY

Clifton Compound

7:00 p.m.

"Who are you and what do you want?"

The man spun toward Tracy and unclasped his hands. He held them out in front of him in a *don't shoot* posture. His blond beard twitched as he smiled. "Whoa, there. I don't deserve the cavalry."

She took aim at his chest. "You didn't answer my question."

"Forgive me, but you're the one pointing the gun."

Tracy scanned the area behind the interloper for others. Either he was alone, or they hid themselves well. No movement caught her eye. She brought her attention back to the man, hostility narrowing her vision. "Answer my question or you'll find out why."

His face brightened into a smile that seemed genuine, but out of place. "A real firecracker, aren't ya?"

"Answer the woman or get off my property." Anne emerged from the other side of the cabin wielding a 12-gauge shotgun. She pressed the butt tight to her shoulder as she came to a stop ten feet from Tracy. "Now."

"My lucky day. Two lovely ladies." The man bent at the waist and twirled his hand in a flourish. "Hampton Rhodes at your service."

Tracy cast a sideways glance at Anne. The other woman didn't back down. If anything, she gripped the shotgun even tighter.

"Where are you from?"

"Oh, here and there."

Anne motioned with her shotgun. "Not good enough."

Hampton sighed and ran a hand through his spiky blond hair. "Well, before the EMP I guess you could say I lived in Tahoe, but I never stayed in one place all that long."

A drifter. Great. Tracy took a step closer. "You need to leave. This is private property."

He made a show of looking around with wide eyes. "I don't see a sign."

"Aren't the two guns pointed at you enough?" Anne widened her stance and took aim. Her gray curls fell in front of her face, but it didn't matter. Tracy got the point.

"You heard the woman. Go. Now."

Hampton chuckled. "Or what? You'll shoot me?"

"You're damn right." Tracy wanted so badly to drop him where he stood, but so far he hadn't done anything except rub her the wrong way.

"This is your last chance. Leave or we'll have no choice."

He took a step back, but no more. "Don't you even want to know why I'm here?"

Shit. Tracy ground her teeth together. The bastard was baiting them. For all they knew he could have twenty friends waiting half a mile away, ready to storm in and take over. "We don't care and we're done waiting."

"What if I told you I'm only a messenger?"

Tracy's lips thinned into a line. If this were her cabin and her property, that would be the end of it. But she couldn't make the choice for Anne.

Anne raised her head a fraction. "I'm listening."

Hampton ran his fingers over his lips and glanced at each woman. "You two know how to put the fear of God in a man, don't you?"

"God has nothing to do with this." Tracy could barely contain the rising anger. He was a swindler and a con-artist. She knew the type. He was the same kind of man who would woo a woman with promises of forever only to disappear the morning after and never call again.

He turned to Anne. "Lake Tahoe's a bit crowded these days. Seems there's all sorts of people fleeing Reno and Sparks and heading for the clear blue waters."

"Your point?"

He glanced around and took in the three buildings

and the work done to the place. "A stranger could be looking for somewhere else to make camp. Somewhere a lot like this."

"Are you saying you're here to rob us?"

Hampton palmed his chest, eyes wide and innocent. "Me? Heavens no. Like I said, I'm just the messenger."

"And who would the message be from?"

He grinned at Tracy and showed off a row of perfect white teeth. "Well, that's not really my place to say."

Anne stepped forward. "We can make you answer."

The smile slid into a smirk. "Dead men can't tell secrets."

Anne motioned to Tracy. "Frisk him. I'll keep watch."

Tracy stepped forward, making sure to stay clear of the direct line between Anne's shotgun and the man's chest. Pulling the handgun tight against her chest to protect it, Tracy stopped a foot from the man. Up close he stank of life on the road or in the woods. His beard covered hollow cheeks and the glint in his eyes she had taken for amusement might have been hunger.

Desperation.

She leaned in and reached for his shoulder. He jerked away.

"Don't do that again." Anne's admonition stilled the man's movement.

Tracy tried again. Her hand connected with his chest and he smiled again. He leaned toward her, pressing his weight into her palm. "Like what you feel?"

Something inside Tracy snapped. She couldn't stand

there and pat this man down when he could be buying time for his buddies. They needed to immobilize the threat he posed and get out there into the woods. Darkness closed in around them with every ticking minute.

Within the hour, it would be pitch black. They would be vulnerable. Exposed.

She curved her lips into a smile and leaned toward him. "Guess it's your lucky day."

"It is?" He brightened.

"Yep. You get to stay the night." In one fluid motion, Tracy brought the gun up with her right hand and slammed the butt of it into the side of the man's head.

He crumpled to the ground. Tracy bent to search for weapons. All she came up with was grimy clothes and empty pockets. "He's clean."

Anne advanced, shotgun still ready to fire.

"Sorry I knocked him out. He gave me the creeps."

"No apologies necessary. He wasn't leaving of his own accord, that was clear."

"What do we do with him?"

Anne stared down at the unconscious man.

"Mom!" Madison's voice rang out from across the property. "Mom are you all right?"

Madison, Brianna, and Peyton ran into the clearing in front of the main cabin, stuttering to a stop when they spotted the man.

Brianna rushed up with a handgun drawn and ready. "We came back and you weren't at the compost pile. When I saw the shovel on the ground, I thought the worst."

Anne smiled. "We're okay. This guy, however, is in a bit of trouble."

"Who is he?"

Tracy snorted. "Claims his name is Hampton Rhodes. Said he was a messenger."

Madison's mouth fell open. "Are we under attack?"

"I don't know." Anne turned to her with a smile. "Find some rope and a dishtowel in the supply cabinet. We can tie him up and gag him for now."

Madison ran toward the cabin and Anne turned to Peyton and Brianna. "Start a patrol of the perimeter now."

"What do we do if we find someone?"

Anne glanced at Tracy before responding. "Shoot on sight."

DAY FORTY-FOUR

CHAPTER SIX

DANI

Northern California Forest
7:30 a.m.

The damp, never-ending rain of the last few days turned the crunchy forest floor into a soft, mushy carpet beneath Dani's feet. Mushrooms popped up on rotting logs and under canopies of ferns, but Dani refused to pick them.

One wrong guess and she'd be dead as a doornail. Nope, mushrooms weren't her thing. Neither was begging a home from yet another family.

A tangle of fallen tree branches blocked her way and Dani kicked at them absently, splintering the soaked wood. Creepy, crawly bugs of all sorts scurried away from her wrath and Larkin snorted beside her.

"What?" She glowered up at the army major. "It was in the way."

"You vertically challenged all of a sudden? It's not like you couldn't have stepped over it."

Just for that Dani stomped on the next clump of logs, but instead of disintegrating, they rolled and slipped and Dani lost her balance. She landed hard on the moist ground and the cool wet soaked through her jeans before she could clamber up.

Damn it.

She wiped at the wet spots on her behind while Larkin laughed into his hand.

"It's not funny."

"Is, too."

For a military man, he sure liked to poke fun. "Why is everything a joke to you?"

"Because what's good living if you can't make light of it?" His smile faded as she fell back into step behind him. He leaned closer. "You gonna tell me about it?"

"What good will that do?"

He shrugged as he walked. "Maybe nothing. But I'm a decent listener."

Dani frowned. She didn't want to discuss her dilemma with anyone, especially not a guy who didn't seem to care where he went as long as he could laugh along the way. But keeping it all bottled in hadn't done much good, either.

After traipsing through the brush and trees in silence for a few minutes, Dani caved. "I don't think we should go with Walter to his cabin."

"Why not?"

"Because every time we try to make friends, they die."

"I'm not dead yet."

Dani cut him a glance. "One out of eight isn't the best odds."

"True. But you have to stop blaming yourself."

Dani stopped and threw up her hands. "Would you cut it out? I'm so sick of everyone telling me what not to feel and how not to think. You can sugarcoat it all you want, but Gloria, Harvey, and Will are dead because we showed up at their house. Melody and Doug are dead because we dragged them into a fight that wasn't theirs to begin with."

Larkin stood beside Dani, not saying a word. His lips pressed together like the cover of a hardback book, straight and unyielding. Dani shook her head in disgust and resumed the walk to the Camaro. Walter could have it for all she cared.

"What would you have done differently?"

The question startled Dani and she glanced over at Larkin. "When?"

"Ever since the EMP. If you're so convinced all these people died because of your actions, looking back, what would you change?"

Dani inhaled and thought about everything that happened, from sneaking out of Gran's room to Colt rescuing her from the national guardsman in the street. If they had left right then, Jarvis wouldn't have known who they were. They could have walked out of Eugene and never looked back.

But that would have meant leaving her grandmother alone in the nursing home. Something Dani would never have done. She sighed. "Nothing. But that doesn't change anything."

Larkin slowed and Dani glanced up. His brows hid the blue of his eyes and his bent head forecast troubled thoughts. "We're all responsible, Dani. Not just you or Colt. We all had a role to play in their deaths. But it's the past and we need to carry on. Not just for all the people we've lost, but for the future."

Her lip slipped between her teeth and Dani nibbled on the chapped skin.

"We need to find a way to survive so we can rebuild. This can't be the end of our country as we know it."

Dani was less concerned about the millions of people in the United States who never even knew she existed than she was about making through the next few days alive. That's all life had ever been to her: a series of struggles, one after the next, with no long-term vision allowed. How could she think about stitching a country back together when they weren't sure where to go or how to get there?

Trekking all the way to Walter's cabin to only turn around and leave again would waste time they didn't have. Dani kept walking, but she couldn't talk to Larkin about the future. She needed time to think through her options and what she would say to Colt to convince him to tell Walter goodbye.

An electronic beep sounded out of a thicket of brambles and Dani jumped. Larkin walked up to the mess with the Camaro's car keys in his hand. "Help me out, will you?"

Together they pulled away branches and thorny

vines and all manner of debris to reveal a mud-covered silver Camaro. "I couldn't even see it under there. How did you hide it?"

Larkin smiled. "Drove it off the road and dragged all that stuff on top of it. Not too hard."

Dani swallowed. This was it. As soon as they got inside and drove it back onto the road, they would be on their way to pick up Colt and Walter, and any chance of setting off on their own would be over. She stared at the passenger-side door.

"Do you know how to drive?"

She nodded. "I hot-wired the pickup, remember?"

"And drove it straight to us. Right." Larkin held out the keys. "Then I have an offer."

Dani raised an eyebrow.

"If you don't want to go with us to Walter's cabin, then don't. Take the keys and the car and go."

Her eyes went wide. "What?"

"You heard me. If you want to leave so bad, do it. You can have the Camaro. Drive it as far as the gas will allow. Get yourself somewhere safe where you can build a life."

Dani shook her head. "I can't take the car. What will you do?"

"Walk. It's what Walter planned to do from the beginning." He thrust the keys out to her. "Take them and go. You'll be free."

Dani reached for the keys, but she hesitated with her fingers still an inch away. Ever since Colt rescued her on the streets of Eugene, he'd stayed by her side. No matter the obstacle or the danger.

The man broke into an apartment full of soldiers and jumped from the three-story window to save her. And she was going to leave without saying goodbye?

As much as she wanted to, Dani couldn't take the keys. She couldn't walk away from the only man who ever gave a damn about her. She owed him more than that.

Dani dropped her hand. "I can't do it. I can't leave like this."

Larkin pulled the keys back. "So you'll go with us?"

After a moment, Dani nodded.

"Atta girl." Larkin reached out and gave her shoulder a pat. "Now let's load up and meet Colt and Walter on the road."

* * *

9:30 A.M.

LARKIN PULLED THE CAMARO OVER TO THE DESIGNATED spot just off the state road. Dani peered into the forest, waiting. "Where are they?"

"It's a lot to carry. That skid can only go so fast. With the soggy ground, they could have gotten stuck."

Dani reached for the door handle. "We should go find them."

"Someone needs to stay with the car."

"You stay. I'll go." She shoved the passenger door open, but Larkin grabbed her by the arm.

"No. You stay. I've got fifty pounds on you at least."

She pursed her lips. "So what?"

"I can bench press you with one hand. Let me do the heavy lifting."

Dani pouted. "Fine. But I'm coming after you if you're not back in half an hour."

Larkin grinned. "Deal."

He clambered out the driver's side and turned to lean back into the car. "Get in the driver's seat. If you see anyone coming, drive."

"Where to?"

"Anywhere they can't catch you."

Dani nodded before watching Larkin walk away. As his lumbering shape disappeared through trees, she thought again about his offer. She had a running car, a handgun tucked in her belt, and a rifle in the backseat.

She glanced at the dash. *It was 109 miles to empty.* She could make it all the way to Lake Tahoe. Somewhere no one knew her and no one counted on her for anything.

Part of her shouted inside her head, *"Go, go!"* Did she really owe Colt? Did she really need to stay?

The other part of her couldn't bear the thought. No matter how much she denied it, no matter how independent and cold she wished she could be, Dani loved Colt. She couldn't leave him even if it was the right thing to do.

Not now. Not ever.

Movement caught her eye and a muddy Colt and Larkin emerged from the tree line. Their arms braced heavy logs on their shoulders, weighed down by a skid full of dehydrated meat and preserved roots and plants and a million other things. Walter came behind, lifting the rear of the skid as best he could to elevate the logs out of the worst of the wet.

They were a sorry sight, sweaty and exhausted and covered in dirt. But Dani couldn't leave them. It might be the worst decision of her life, but she'd see Walter to his cabin. After that, all bets were off. She rolled down the passenger-side window and leaned over. "You fellas need a ride?"

CHAPTER SEVEN

MADISON

Mud squelched through the lugs of Madison's boots as she stalked through the forest. All night the three college kids took turns keeping watch, one canvassing the front of the property, one the back, and one asleep. Each one slept in fits and starts for a few hours, but it was enough.

Madison couldn't sleep any longer if her life depended on it. Not when a group of interlopers could be plotting right now how to tear the Clifton property apart. She shook her head at her foolish actions over the past two weeks.

When they arrived at Brianna's family compound, relief consumed Madison. They were safe. Secure. Home. But it was all a fantasy.

No one would ever be safe again. Why had she let herself believe that? Madison stomped in frustration. Two weeks and she'd gone soft.

Shoving the anger aside, she focused on the task at hand: clearing the forest. At first light, she'd woken up Brianna and along with Peyton the three of them set off to search the surrounding area for any sign of Hampton's crew.

The man couldn't be alone. Based on what he'd told her mom, there could be a whole gang of people hiding and waiting. If they were lurking in her section of the forest, Madison would find them. She wouldn't let them hurt her family or Brianna's.

Early morning light filtered through the trees, shafts of warm yellows and oranges lighting up the forest floor and casting shadows beneath the new leaves. Any other day and Madison would stop to enjoy the stillness and the beauty of it all. Nature, unadulterated and serene.

But danger lurked behind every hardwood and around every bed of brambles. Madison checked the safety on her rifle before easing around a thicket of wild blackberries. White flowers and small green lumps dotted the vines. In a few weeks, the bushes would be covered with thick, ripe berries.

Her mouth watered at the thought. Jam, pie, juice. The possibilities were endless.

Madison cleared the bush and moved on, working in ever-increasing circles away from the cabins and the main portion of the Clifton property. Soon she would reach the end of their land and the start of the national forest.

Part of the allure of the property the Cliftons owned were the three sides of national forest land as its border. Fences might have made good neighbors before the grid collapse, but no neighbors was better now.

At the edge of a steep grade, Madison paused. Leaves and pebbles skittered down the slope into a gulley at the basin. Where Sacramento and Davis were flat and endless, the foothills were full of hills and valleys and hidden dangers. Crouching low, Madison braced herself on the edge of the slope before easing forward.

Her heels slipped on the loose debris and she skittered a few feet. Her heel caught on an exposed root and Madison lunged for something to hold onto. She scrabbled for a branch, a twig, a winding root. Anything.

Nothing gave her purchase. She slid more. One foot, then two, faster and faster until too many trees to count passed her by.

The ravine kept going and going on down below her, at least thirty feet. *I can't fall. Not from here.*

Madison leaned back, twisting and shifting her weight onto her backside, trying in vain to stop the slide. The rifle hampered her efforts, but Madison couldn't let go. She had to stop herself.

The slope veered straighter and straighter and Madison picked up speed. She would die falling down this ravine. One stupid decision to slide down a hill and she wouldn't ever make it home to see her parents, pet Fireball, or thank Brianna for saving her life.

No.

She couldn't let that happen. Rock emerged from

the dirt-covered slope and Madison angled for it, digging her nails into the pocked surface.

Her fingers found a crevice and Madison shoved them inside, hanging on with all her strength and wincing as her body slipped below the rock.

She dangled from the edge, four fingers away from free fall. What appeared to be a shallow gulley from the top of the ridge was in fact a massive crevasse with rocks and water and nothing but sharp edges and slick surfaces.

Her grip on the rock loosened and Madison swallowed. She couldn't pull herself up with one hand. The rifle would have to go.

She cursed herself for not taking the gun with the shoulder strap. With an anguished gasp, Madison dropped the rifle. It clattered to the ground amongst the rocks below, but she didn't watch.

Inhaling as deep a breath as she could muster, Madison tightened all her muscles and swung her free arm up to the rock. She grabbed ahold of the same gap her other hand clung to and heaved.

Her biceps burned, her abs screamed, but little by little she pulled herself up. First one forearm, then the other, belly scraping against the rock face, feet clambering onto the surface.

She collapsed against the side of the slope, panting and begging for oxygen. The boulder was barely big enough to sit upon, but it saved her life. Madison sucked in breath after breath until she could breathe and her muscles stopped burning.

After a few minutes, she risked a glance over the side

of the rock. Her rifle lay in the shallow water twenty feet straight down. Thanks to the angle of the hill, she hadn't seen the sheer drop from her vantage point on top. But now it was plain: she was lucky to be alive.

Madison glanced up. The top of the ridge looked so far away. How would she ever claw her way back up?

She frowned. *I can do this. I'm tougher than some hill in the woods.*

Gritting her teeth, she eased up onto her feet and stretched up the slope. It wasn't all that different from the rock wall she'd climbed at the college gym. Only this wall was covered in leaves and dirt and loose rocks.

Madison reached for a rock to pull herself up, but it crumbled away in her hand. She grabbed at a root, but yanked it out of the dirt before she could climb a single foot.

Damn it.

Using the toe of her boot, she tried another tactic: digging her own hold. Once her foot disappeared inside a wedge of dirt, Madison eased up onto the ball of her foot. It held.

She tried again with the other foot a bit higher, kicking at the slope until the debris fell away and she exposed a sturdy little ledge.

Agonizingly slowly she ascended, one kicked-in ledge at a time. Her fingernails ripped and tore as she dug at the dirt to give purchase to her hands. Mud soaked through her jeans and coated her face and neck.

But still she climbed. Up and up until at last, level forest floor rewarded her efforts. She heaved herself over the ledge, slipping on the leaves in her haste. It took the last surge of strength from deep within her core to scale the edge, but Madison prevailed.

She kissed the ground beneath her face as tears of exhaustion mixed with the dirt on her cheeks. Nature didn't win.

Madison flopped over onto her back and laughed through the tears. *I did it. I really did it.*

She closed her eyes and thanked everyone from God to her yoga instructor on campus to her dad for forcing her to accept the boots Brianna offered upon their arrival.

When leaves crunched nearby, Madison didn't hear them. She was too busy congratulating herself on surviving.

When a twig snapped ten feet away, she blew it off as a squirrel or a bird.

When a pair of boots stopped beside her head, she blinked.

A scream bubbled up her throat and Madison scrambled to escape. It was too late.

The rock slammed into the side of her head and the darkness took over.

CHAPTER EIGHT

TRACY

CLIFTON COMPOUND
7:30 a.m.

TRACY RUBBED AT HER PUFFY EYES. IT HAD BEEN A LONG night standing watch over the intruder's unconscious body, but Tracy couldn't trust anyone else. After what happened all those weeks ago in Sacramento, she refused to take the chance.

The door to the cabin opened and Anne poked her head inside. One look at Tracy and she stepped in and closed the door. "Have you been here all night?"

Tracy pushed back a lock of hair and nodded. "We can't let him out of our sight. Not for a minute."

"You should have woken me or traded shifts with Peyton."

"No. I'm not leaving this asshole for a minute."

Anne's brow knit as she stared at the unconscious

man trussed up in a kitchen chair. "How about you go to sleep now? I'll take over and watch him until the kids get back."

Tracy shook her head once in a firm denial. "Not a chance. No one is dying today because of me."

With a frown, Anne walked over to the counter. "If you're going to be that stubborn about it, then I'm making coffee. We can watch him breathe together."

She busied herself with scooping a spoonful of instant coffee into two mugs and filling a pot with water. Thanks to a deep, private well, the Cliftons had access to all the fresh water they could need and then some. One of the many things Tracy was so thankful for now.

No man wandering in with a smile on his face would stab them in the back and ruin what they started here. She'd learned from the last few weeks. Strangers couldn't be trusted. People lied.

Anne walked the pot of water over to the wood-burning stove and set it on the front burner. After adding another log to the fire and poking the burning embers around until the wood caught, she turned to face Tracy. At forty-four years old, Anne Clifton was almost Tracy's age, but instead of downsizing into a little house in town and relaxing with her daughter off in college, Anne had spent the last five years turning this secluded property in the foothills into a homestead.

With a deep well, solar panels on the roof, and enough firewood to last a year, they were self-sufficient and well prepared to ride out the chaos brewing in the rest of the country. Tracy wished she had been so thoughtful and forward-looking. Instead of worrying about the end of the modern world, she'd been too busy planning things to do in retirement and enjoying her job at the library.

What a waste.

She snorted in disgust at herself as she turned back to the man calling himself Hampton. If he was being honest before, then where were his friends? Was he really there to scope the place out or was he just a crazy man wandering the woods alone?

Tracy jumped when a steaming cup of coffee appeared in front of her. She smiled up at Anne. "Thanks."

Anne pulled out a chair and planted it next to Tracy. "Now talk."

"About what?"

"Why you won't leave this guy's side. He's been unconscious for hours. You clocked him so hard he probably won't remember his name when he finally wakes up. So spill. You don't seem like the type to shoot first and ask questions later."

"I didn't shoot him."

Anne pinned her with a look and Tracy caved. "I've been here before and last time it didn't go so well." She sipped her coffee and leaned back before filling Anne in on the details of their flight from Sacramento.

"It got that bad, that fast?"

Tracy nodded. "As soon as Bill discovered that I stockpiled the day the EMP hit, he turned on me. I can't prove that he's the one who started the fire, but—"

"Why didn't you kill him?"

Tracy focused on the ground. "I wish I had. But

once Wanda died, it all devolved into chaos. First the gunfight and then the fire. I burned my hand terribly." Tracy held up her palm and showed Anne the scars snaking across her palm. The skin would be pink and angry for months, but at least she'd survived.

"I had an infection and the pain made me delirious. I actually don't even remember what happened after that." She tucked her head toward her chin. "I left my daughter to shoulder the burden of escaping that place all on her own."

Anne reached out and squeezed Tracy's arm. "Our children are capable of more than we give them credit for."

"I know. They're amazing women."

"Peyton's not bad either."

Tracy explained Peyton's lack of a family and how his father had disowned him just before the EMP. The boy had been a quasi-son to her ever since Madison met him at UC Davis; now it was all but legal. He would be a part of their family forever.

She glanced at Anne. "When did you leave home? Stockton's a farther trek than Sacramento."

Anne blew on the top of her coffee and drank a little before responding. "We left as soon as Barry got off work. His boss wouldn't let him go early." She wrinkled her nose at the memory. "I told him what did it matter when there wouldn't be a job to go back to, but the man has principles."

Tracy smiled. "Sounds like my husband." Walter had done his duty and boarded a plane headed to Seattle and Hong Kong despite seeing the warnings. If he'd shirked his duty, he would have been home to help defend their property. So many things would have been different.

"Our husbands have convictions. That's what makes them good people."

Anne nodded. "I know. But it sure would have saved some hassle. We lost an entire carload of supplies on the way and almost didn't make it here."

Tracy remembered their attempt to load up at Walmart and the two men more interested in target practice than long-term survival. Although they all escaped that day, they weren't so lucky at the farm in Chico. Tucker's loss still stung. She leaned closer to Anne. "I'm sorry we lost Tucker."

"So am I. Brianna won't talk to me about him, but I know she's still grieving."

"We all are. Tucker was a good young man. He deserved better."

The pair of women lapsed into silence while they thought about the struggles of the past six weeks. So many people had died. Not just Wanda and Tucker, but all the people Tracy and her family had killed. The men at the house in Chico. The thugs hiding inside the college building. The attack at the farm.

She closed her eyes for a moment and inhaled. Would Hampton be another? She opened her eyes and focused on the man. Unconscious, he didn't seem so scary. Battered coat with a few rips and tears. Boots caked in mud. Jeans turned dingy brown from dirt and nonstop wear.

Leaning forward, she sniffed at him. The stench of

man too long without a shower. If he did belong to a group of people, they weren't living the life of luxury. That made them dangerous.

She checked the paracord looped around his wrists and ankles. Peyton had done a good job trussing him up. The man wasn't going anywhere unless he was a contortionist in his prior life.

"You think he's a threat?"

Tracy hesitated. "I don't know. But I'm not willing to take the chance. As soon as he wakes up, we're finding out what he knows and who he's with, no matter what."

"Barry should be home soon. We could wait for him."

"No. The longer we wait, the riskier the situation becomes. We need to eliminate the threat as soon as possible."

"If there's someone nearby, the kids will flush them out."

Tracy nodded. Since they hadn't come back with news, she assumed they were safe. With three of them out there and enough firepower to take down a small army, Tracy didn't worry about the day ahead. It was the next few days and weeks that gave her concern.

More people like Hampton would be coming. More people would try to take what they had. "We need to step up the perimeter defenses. Fortify this place for attack."

Anne sat a bit straighter in the chair. "I've come to the same conclusion. We hoped when we picked this property that we were far enough off the beaten path and no one would happen upon us by accident."

"Guess nowhere is remote enough."

"I suppose you're right." Anne shook her head. "I never thought things would get this bad, this fast. Riots in all the major cities? No emergency relief anywhere? I'd hoped most of the urbanites would just stay put and survive off rations supplied by the local government."

"No one anticipated this kind of chaos. We've been comfortable for too long."

Anne nodded.

Tracy opened her mouth to say more when the front door slammed open. An out-of-breath Peyton stood on the front step, eyes wide and full of fear and anger.

"What is it? What's wrong?"

Peyton sucked in a breath and gripped the doorframe for support. "It's Madison. We've looked everywhere, but we can't find her."

Tracy stood up in alarm and the coffee sloshed in her cup. "What do you mean?"

"She's gone."

"That's impossible. Maybe she's just out farther than normal or she's down in a gulley you haven't checked."

Peyton shook his head. "I don't think so. I think someone took her."

Brianna thundered up the front steps and squeezed past Peyton to enter the cabin. "He's right. Madison's been kidnapped." She held up a rifle slick with water and mud. "I found her weapon in a creek bed. There was a pool of blood on the leaves at the top."

Tracy staggered back. *Not Madison. Not my daughter.* She spun on her heel. Hampton needed to wake up. *Right this minute.*

CHAPTER NINE

WALTER

Northern California Forest
12:00 p.m.

The Camaro crawled down the road. Thanks to the gear lashed to the roof, they could barely drive faster than they could walk, but it sure beat carrying the load. Walter checked the rearview and the side mirrors every minute or so, ensuring they were alone.

With thirty road miles separating them from the Cliftons' cabin, it would take them all day to get there at this pace. Before, the separation didn't bother him, but ever since he made the decision to head home, anxiety crept beneath his calm. He wanted to be there yesterday.

Before the EMP he made his living flying people all over the world. Sitting in a cockpit looking down over the specks of houses and the vastness of America brought him peace. Now traveling only gave him heart palpitations and a cold sweat.

At least he was bringing home more than venison jerky and ginseng root. He glanced at Larkin beside him in the front seat. He brought muscle and manpower and fighting skills.

The Cliftons had the property and the buildings and the setup to survive in a civilized world, but that world died six weeks ago. Every day that went by brought more desperation and lawlessness. More risk and outside threats. Someone would come to take what they had.

With Colt and Larkin by his side, Walter could defend the property. He could keep his wife and daughter safe.

Tilting the rearview, Walter caught a glimpse of Colt, Dani, and little Lottie in the backseat. Trained a SEAL, Colt could still catch a few minutes of sleep anywhere, anytime. Apparently he'd taught Dani the same thing. The three of them made an unlikely family —gruff middle-aged man, teenage orphan, and a little Yorkie. But it worked.

Larkin adjusted in his seat. "You really think you can survive out here in a cabin long-term?"

Walter glanced over at the man. About his age, career army, no ring on his finger. A solitary man, Walter guessed. He nodded as he turned back to the road. "I think so. As long as we can defend it."

"That's the hardest part, isn't it? Defense? Not just from outsiders, though."

"What do you mean?"

Larkin exhaled and ruffed up his beard. "There's no

peace anymore. Never a chance to relax and let down your guard. We're living in a war zone. That does things to people."

Thanks to Colt, Walter knew a bit about what transpired in Eugene, but not a lot. "Are you talking about the rest of your group?"

"Partly. But not just them. Everyone reacts differently to this sort of stress. We're not a bunch of soldiers sent halfway around the world to fight in someone else's backyard. This is our land. Our home. And it's not under attack from some foreign invader. We're tearing ourselves apart."

Walter blinked. "Not everyone is like that."

"Not everyone, but enough." Larkin turned to look out the window. "Melody Harper was a good woman. She didn't deserve to die alone in the woods."

"Colt said she fell. It was an accident."

"The car crash tore her apart. She'd lost her home, her life in Eugene, and then to watch as the Wilkinses died in front of her..." He shook his head. "She couldn't handle it. Neither could her brother."

"The man I killed."

Larkin nodded.

"I'm sorry, Larkin. It was a snap judgment. I thought he was going to kill someone."

"You did the right thing. But I wish it hadn't come to that." He turned back to Walter with a sad smile. "I thought Melody might be the one."

Walter kept his expression even. He didn't know what he would do if he lost Tracy or his daughter. "I didn't know. I'm sorry for your loss."

"Me, too. But that seems to be my track record. Every girl I meet either dies or disappears." He leaned back in the seat and tapped his fingers on the ledge of the door. "First girl I ever loved went to Haiti on a mission trip and never came home."

"What happened to her?"

"Don't know. Her father was a pastor in the local church. He took his whole family to Haiti every year to build houses and a school and spread the word of God as he put it. One day she didn't show up for dinner."

"Any trace of her?"

"Not a one. I was seventeen and head over heels for her. Janie Kester. Red hair, green eyes, dimple on her left cheek that only showed up when she laughed. Most beautiful girl in all of Westfield High."

Larkin exhaled a heavy, pendulous breath laced with grief. "I didn't find out until the first day of my junior year." He shook his head at the memory. "There I was, this gangly, uncoordinated boy standing by the front entrance of school with a rose in my hand, waiting. I stood there until halfway through first period. The principal came out and told me."

"What about her family?"

"They stayed in Haiti for months afterward. When they finally came home, her father couldn't even look me in the eye. So much for God taking care of his own."

Silence filled the car. Walter could understand how an experience like that could transform a man, let alone a kid.

"Ever since then, I haven't put much stock in love or

God or fate." He paused and his next words came out rough and tortured. "Until Melody."

Walter had met Tracy around the same time as Larkin met his Janie. What would have happened if he'd lost her all those years ago? Would he still be the man he was today without Tracy by his side, growing and changing and loving him for more than half his life?

Not a chance. He owed his sanity to that woman. Tracy gave him the strength to make the hard choices. Larkin had been forced to make them on his own.

Walter had a newfound appreciation for the man. "When did you join the army?"

"I enlisted as soon as I could. I had to get out of that town. After my first tour, I used the GI Bill to get my degree and became an officer. I would have stayed active duty if I hadn't broken my back. Turns out they don't want majors with fused vertebrae on the front lines."

Walter nodded. The transition to National Guard made sense. So did Larkin's take-no-prisoners attitude. "I'd be honored to have you stick around, Larkin. We could use you at the cabin."

"You mean you can use my jaded lack of compassion?"

Walter smiled at the man. "Exactly."

They shared a small laugh. "You really think they'll take us all in?"

"I can make the case. No guarantees, but once Barry and Anne see what you can offer, I can't imagine them saying no. They need protection. We all do."

They lapsed into silence and Walter concentrated on the road. At least the conversation with Larkin distracted Walter from the snail's pace. They were still fifteen miles from the turnout to the gravel road. Sill so far from his wife and daughter.

He craned his neck toward the window to catch a glimpse of the load on the roof. The logs wobbled as they drove and the tarp flapped in the wind, but it all appeared secure. He leaned back up just as Larkin jerked upright.

"Walter! Stop! There's something in the road."

Walter pressed the brakes, but with the load on top, he couldn't stop on a dime. Everything would fly off the top.

The car slowed as Walter squinted to make out what Larkin saw. The sun glinted off something on the asphalt and Walter swerved. The gear on the roof slid to the side and Lottie barked in the back seat.

Colt spoke up from the back, wide awake in an instant. "What's going on?"

"Something in the road. Looked like metal. I think Walter dodged it."

Walter glanced at the dash. A red warning light flashed. "Don't celebrate yet." He slowed the car to a stop on the side of the road. "Cover me."

He opened the door to the car as Larkin did the same. The army major propped a rifle on the hood and surveyed the road. "Looks clear."

Walter eased out and crouched beside the front left tire. The sound of whooshing air greeted him and the tire sagged before his eyes. *Damn it.* He eased around the front of the car and checked the other tire. Three gleaming bright nails stuck out of the tire as the rubber slumped against the road.

One flat they could manage. Two? Not possible. He pulled the handgun from his waist and crept back past the edge of the car. Larkin got out and eased to a shooting position behind the door.

It didn't take long for Walter to find them. Strips of nails from an automatic nail gun sprawled across both lanes of the rural state road. Their tire tracks were the only disturbance. He rushed back to the car and clambered inside.

Colt spoke up before he could. "It's an ambush, isn't it?"

Walter nodded. "Strips of nails across the road. Whoever put them there hoped for a situation just like this."

Dani shifted in the backseat. "Then where are they? Why aren't they shooting?"

"They expected us to be going a hell of a lot faster." Colt pointed at the curve up ahead. "Most people would be driving, what? Sixty miles an hour? Anyone who hit those nails at such a speed would lose control and slam into those trees before they could stop."

Larkin agreed. "Whoever planted this expected to reap the rewards without getting their hands dirty. They could ransack the vehicle after everyone inside died."

"What are we going to do?"

Walter glanced at Dani before turning to Colt. "We should give them exactly what they're expecting."

CHAPTER TEN

COLT

Northern California Forest
2:00 p.m.

Colt shoved a rock onto the gas pedal of the Camaro and leaned over to shift the car into drive. He ducked out of the way as the car took off on two flat tires and a whole lot of giddy-up. Thanks to the horsepower, it sped down the asphalt despite the drag from the flat rubber and slammed into the bank of trees with tremendous force.

The hood crumpled, glass shattered, and by the time it came to rest, nothing was left of the front of the vehicle. It would take whoever set the trap hours to discover no one was inside. And even if they did, the few bits of gear they staged in the back seat might distract them long enough for Colt and the rest of them to get far enough away to not be found.

He walked back to Dani and Lottie and tried to shake off his frustration. Ever since he left the University of Oregon campus, he hadn't caught a break. Dani had been kidnapped and attacked and shot. Colt hadn't fared much better.

Between the two of them, they'd killed more men than Colt wanted to count and left just as many to die in agony. The last few weeks had been as brutal as any he'd seen in combat, if not in intensity, than in emotional toll. There was something different about fighting civilians.

They weren't there to kill you because that was their job. They just wanted to survive like everyone else. He forced a smile onto his face. "Ready to drag a bunch of gear twenty miles?"

Dani smirked. "Don't think we have a choice."

With their packs loaded up with as much as they could carry before the straps tore, the skid was reduced to a still heavy, but manageable load. Colt took the left and Larkin the right with Walter, Dani, and little Lottie leading the way. They planned to switch every mile.

The log dug into Colt's shoulder as he adjusted his position. Every step took concentrated effort. After a quarter mile his back ached. After a half a mile, his bad knee threatened to buckle.

Larkin grunted beside him. "I'm too old for this."

Colt snorted out a laugh. "Tell me about it. My knee's about to give out."

"My back's not too happy, either," Larkin groaned as he exhaled. "No one ever told me in the apocalypse I'd regret spinal fusion surgery."

At their complaining, Walter left his position on

patrol and took up the rear, easing a bit of the burden, but not nearly enough.

The end of the first mile, Colt set his side on the ground and shrugged off the pack. He collapsed onto the earth and winced as his knee popped. "We'll never be able to do this for twenty miles."

Larkin almost fell to the ground beside him, stretching out like a kid about to make a snow angel. "This is why men our age retire from the military."

Walter crouched between them both. "You're right. I miscalculated. The load is too heavy."

Colt tilted his head. "Any bright ideas on what to do with it all?"

"We'll have to hide it and come back for it later. One of the kids has a Jeep. If we can clear enough of a path through the woods, we can four-wheel here without getting on the main road."

Walter stood up and surveyed the pile of supplies.

With a grunt, Colt forced himself up to sit. The prospect of not carrying the skid gave him a surge of energy. "We'll have to dig another hole and bury it all."

"It's like I'm back in the Marine Corps and out on a training mission."

Larkin sat up with a wince. "Right. Like you ever dug fighting holes as an officer."

Walter grinned. "I never said I did, but I sure ordered extra military instruction a time or two."

"Bastard. Enlisted guys had to hate you."

"Yeah, but they were damn good with a shovel."

Lottie yipped and all three men turned around.

Dani stood a few feet away with the little dog in her arms. "You three are crazy, you know that?"

Colt rolled over and lifted a shovel from the skid. He held it out to her. "And exhausted. Guess who gets to dig first?"

* * *

5:30 P.M.

COLT GLANCED UP AT THE SKY AND FROWNED. Two hours of solid daylight left at best. They needed to make better time. After digging a hole big enough to store all the gear, the four of them dumped everything inside, used the tarp as a top cover and then loaded the dirt and debris on top.

Scattering leaves and branches over it, Dani and Larkin blended the existing forest floor with the disturbed dirt until no one could tell the difference. Colt notched a mark in four neighboring trees and Walter made a note of their distance from the road and the direction toward the cabin.

It wasn't perfect, but it was the best they could do given the circumstances.

They couldn't risk marking a trail to find their way back in case someone else discovered it and followed it straight back to the cabin. Colt sipped some water from his canteen and chomped off a strip of jerky. At least they weren't hungry or wet.

It could always be worse.

He glanced over at Dani. The girl hadn't complained about taking the laboring oar for digging the hole or hiking with a pack that had to weigh half her body weight or more. She trudged along beside him in silence, eyes open and head scanning the forest ahead.

As long as they were on the move, Dani was the same: confident, prepared, ready to tackle anything. It was when they settled down that she grew restless and unhappy. There was something to be said for the nomad life.

It's what Colt had wanted when he walked out of the University of Oregon and it's what they had now. Maybe staying at the cabin Walter shared with another family wasn't the best choice. Maybe he should take Dani and Lottie and keep moving.

A breeze blew Dani's hair beside him and he shook off the doubts. Traveling by foot through the foothills was no life for a fifteen-year-old girl. They might survive the summer, but what would they do at the first sign of snow? How would they survive when the temperatures dropped below freezing and the animals went into hiding?

If she didn't want to stay with Walter, then the only choice available was to find another town and carve out an existence among the dwindling few still clinging to their old ways of life. It wasn't a future he wanted for Dani or himself.

Colt turned to catch sight of Larkin and Walter behind him. Twenty feet separated the two pairs of hikers, but they were as much of a unit as any he'd had in the military. He knew he could trust the three of them with his life. Larkin had proven himself time and again. Walter had saved Dani's life.

They were good men. He would be honored to spend the rest of his days in their company.

"Colt?"

He spun back around at the tremor in Dani's voice. "What?"

She pointed through a thicket. "Do you see that?"

Squinting, he searched the area. A scrap of orange. A hint of blue. *Human activity.* He motioned with his hand and Larkin hustled up. Colt dropped his voice to a whisper. "There's something out there."

"I'll cover you."

Colt eased his pack to the ground and loped into the thicker brush, navigating through ferns and fallen logs to a little clearing twenty yards away. Beer cans littered the area. A ripped-up sleeping bag covered in leaves was sprawled on the ground. Colt picked up a stick and poked at the orange nylon.

Bears lived in the vicinity, but the slices through the bag didn't look like a vicious animal attack. Straight and long, with nary a jagged edge, they appeared manmade and from a damn sharp knife. He used the stick to flip the bag over.

The bottom was stained a dark brown and Colt recoiled. Blood. A ton of it.

He stood up with a jolt. Whoever had been camping here didn't do so in peace. He looked around for any sign of the wounded person. With that much blood loss, could anyone even escape? If not, where was the body?

Sucking in a breath, he smelled nothing but decaying debris and pine trees.

No stench of death. No hint of the atrocity committed in this little patch of forest. He hustled back to the group and met their waiting stares. "Someone was attacked here. No sign of a body."

Walter inhaled. "We need to get home as quick as we can."

Colt nodded. "The longer we're out here, the riskier it gets."

The setting sun cut through the leaves and lit Colt's hands in an orange glow. "We don't have much daylight left. Let's make the most of it."

As they hiked away from the remains of past violence, Colt glanced behind him. Whoever did that could be lurking just out of sight. Watching and waiting for a chance to strike.

CHAPTER ELEVEN

TRACY

Clifton Compound
10:00 a.m.

Tracy steeled herself for the job ahead. With the kids out on patrol and Anne checking the outbuildings, no one stood between her and Hampton Rhodes. She would find out all of his secrets and plans.

One way or another.

The splash of cold water on his face did nothing. Neither did the constant shaking of his shoulder or the slap across his face. She'd hit him too hard the night before.

No matter. If he didn't wake the easy way, she'd go hard.

The needle sank into his finger like a knife into a ripe tomato; initial resistance, then smooth and steady.

Blood welled on the man's finger pad and his head jerked.

His eyes fluttered and Tracy widened her stance, legs apart, one hand braced on her knee. She sat no more than a foot away, face-to-face with the man who would lead her to her daughter.

She pressed on the bloody finger with the point of the needle and Hampton's eyes popped all the way open. His pupils swelled before contracting and bringing her into focus. He glanced down at his finger and the blood dripping off his skin and tried to jerk his hand away. The paracord held him tight.

"What the hell are you doing?"

Tracy smiled. "Waking you up."

He jerked against the ropes. "My head is killing me."

"That's because I slammed my pistol right about here." Tracy reached out and thumped the swollen lump on the side of his head.

Hampton almost screamed. "You bitch!"

"Seemed only fair. You weren't being the most forthcoming."

"I didn't know you would take me hostage." He tugged on the ropes again. "What's your problem?"

"I need information. Tell me about your group. Now."

"I don't have a group!"

"Liar."

"I'm serious. It's just me."

"Last night you told a different story."

He ran his tongue over his teeth and grimaced. "Last night I was high on oxy. I could have told you the sky was raining marshmallows and the trees were candy canes."

Tracy stared at him. His pupils were dilated maybe more than normal and he trembled a bit as he sat in the chair, but fear could cause the same reaction. He could be lying about the drugs and the rest of his group. "Tell me where your group is hiding."

Hampton threw himself back in the chair. "I don't have a group."

With swift precision, Tracy reached out with the needle and stabbed another one of his fingers.

He screamed, full-throated and terrified.

"Tell me where they are."

"You're crazy."

She leaned close enough to see the flecks of brown in his blue eyes and the fear swelling his pupils. "Yes, I am. And I'm only getting started."

Tracy stood up and walked into the kitchen. The drawer slid open with a long, steady screech.

Hampton jumped. "What are you doing?"

"Picking a knife." She held up two. "Serrated or not?" She turned the two knives around in her hands, focusing on the dips and valleys of the longer blade. "I'm thinking serrated. It'll hurt like a bitch when I carve up your face."

Hampton lunged against the ropes, struggling so violently that the chair bounced up and down. He managed to scoot it back about a foot before Tracy closed the space between them and grabbed him by the shirt.

"Not so fast, pretty boy. I'm about to see what's underneath that beard."

He blubbered at her, stammering as flecks of spittle coated the wiry hairs beneath his lips. "I told you the truth! There is no group!"

Tracy refused to back down. Her daughter was missing. Someone hurt her bad enough to leave a puddle of blood behind. Madison was out there, hurting and desperate to come home. What were the odds more than one group was out there, seeking to harm them?

No cries of innocence would dampen Tracy's resolve. This man would tell her what she wanted to know or he would die right there in Anne Clifton's kitchen.

Maybe it was the grim look of determination in her eyes or the way she advanced on him with the ten-inch bread knife, but at last, he cracked.

"Fine! Fine! I've got a group. But they're not going to hurt anyone. I swear."

Tracy leaned back. "Tell me everything."

Hampton sucked in a breath of air and glanced up at the ceiling. "There's five of us. We live in a cabin on the other side of the creek."

Tracy lunged forward and grabbed a fistful of his beard. She brought the knife up and sliced at his hair, using the point of his chin as a guide. Hampton struggled in her grip, almost falling backward as she cut through the clump of matted tangles.

As he pulled away, blood bloomed on his chin. "Don't lie to me again or next time, I won't be so gentle."

She tossed the handful of beard she'd hacked off his face to the floor. "Try again."

Hampton snuffed up a nose full of snot and scowled. Gone was the fear and the innocent expression. In their place was hard, flinted anger and calculation. "That perfect ponytail and those trim little jeans fooled Eileen, but you're tougher than you look."

Tracy didn't say a word. This was the real Hampton Rhodes. This was the monster lurking beneath the surface. Whoever Eileen was, she couldn't be much better.

"When we first saw you in the forest, we thought you'd be an easy mark. You and that other woman." He sneered at her. "What are you, a couple raising all those teenagers together?"

She didn't take the bait. Instead she plastered a smug smile on her face and played along. "What's it to you? Don't like lesbians?"

"I don't care who you screw. But everybody knows a couple of women without any men around are an easier mark."

She made a show of the knife. "Still think that way?"

He swallowed. "Maybe my attitude's changed a bit."

"Good. Where is your camp?"

"I'm not telling you that."

"How many of you are there?"

"I'm not telling you that, either."

Tracy ground her teeth together. This man was proving more difficult than she wanted. He needed to break already so she could find Madison before they killed her. What if they had a car? What if she was already too far away to find?

She leaned forward again. "How about I start taking fingers? A pinky to start. Work my way over." She grabbed at the hand she'd already stabbed twice with a needle. "I don't see any calluses here. Are you left-handed, Hampton? Or just live a life of luxury?"

He struggled against her, but still refused to talk. After a brief tussle, Tracy leaned back. If fear and pain wouldn't get to him, maybe the truth would.

With a solemn, heavy exhale, Tracy composed herself. She pushed the so-called perfect hair off her face and waited until he looked her in the eye. "I'm not asking you these questions because I want to hurt you or your friends. My daughter is missing. I think your group had something to do with it. Please tell me where they are."

He regarded her for a moment, chest swelling with breath. "If I do?"

"Then I'll find them, have a conversation, and get my daughter back."

"What if it's not that easy?"

"Then it'll be hard."

Hampton lifted his chin, high and defiant despite the circumstances. "Eileen will never let her go without a fight. She set her sights on this place and that woman gets what she wants."

Tracy gripped the knife with a crushing force, but managed to keep it in her lap. "Who's Eileen?"

"The leader of our little group. She doesn't negotiate."

"Tell me where she is and give me a chance. Let me try."

Hampton leaned back with a smug grin, shutting her out. "I don't think so."

Tracy fought the darkness welling up inside her like a turbulent black sea, pungent and thick. "Please, Hampton."

Instead of softening or feeling pity at her plight, Hampton laughed.

The floodgates inside Tracy opened. She would get the information she needed from this man. Her daughter wasn't going to die out there somewhere begging for her life or worse.

A parade of horrible thoughts ran through Tracy's mind. All the things a bastard like Hampton could do to a nineteen-year-old in the woods. If anyone in his group laid a hand on her, they would feel a mother's wrath. Tracy leaned forward with the knife.

The next time Hampton screamed, people would hear it in Lake Tahoe.

She reached for the man's hand when the door to the kitchen cabin burst open. Peyton stood in the threshold. Sweat soaked his shirt, turning the blue fabric almost black.

Tracy twisted around, knife still ready in her hand. "Have you found her?"

"No." Peyton's Adam's apple bobbed as he forced a swallow. "There's no sign of her or anyone else."

Tracy exhaled and stood up.

Hampton immediately began to protest. He shouted at Peyton. "You have to help me! She's crazy. She threatened to break all of my fingers and stab me with that knife!"

Tracy turned back to face him. "Should I start now?"

He stilled and she smiled. "Didn't think so. Now if you'll excuse me a moment." She stood and made her way over to Peyton.

He eyed her with a wary expression. "Are you really going to torture him?"

"If I have to."

"Has he told you anything?"

"Yes and no. He's part of a group and they were casing the place. He thinks it's just us—two women and three kids. An easy mark."

"What will you do to him?"

Tracy turned back and regarded the man she'd knocked unconscious and had been threatening with no success. "Whatever it takes. He *will* take me to Madison."

"And if he can't?"

She spoke loud enough for Hampton to hear. "Then he can die out there and not stain the hardwood floors with his blood."

Peyton's mouth fell open. "Mrs. Sloane... are you ... okay?"

Tracy shook her head. "No, Peyton. I'm not okay. My daughter is gone. I've hit a man upside the head, stabbed him with a needle, and threatened him with torture, but he still won't tell me the truth. But the worst part is that there's no end to any of this. People will always be coming to get us. Someone will always be trying to take what we have."

"The Cliftons didn't."

"No, but look what that got us. We spent two weeks living in paradise and now Madison might be dead."

"You don't know that."

"We don't know anything and that's the problem." She turned back to Hampton. He would tell her the truth, somehow, some way. And if he didn't, she'd kill him. Her voice once again rose to fill the cabin. "Get me a good solid tree branch and strip it, will you, Peyton?"

"What for?"

She smiled at Hampton. "You can't roast a pig without a spit."

CHAPTER TWELVE

TRACY

Clifton Compound

12:00 p.m.

"You can't do this."

Tracy continued cutting lengths of cord to lash Hampton to the mast Peyton dutifully delivered first thing that morning. "I can and I will."

"Tracy. You need to think this through. I know you're hurting right now, but—"

She cut off Brianna's mother mid-sentence. "I am not hurting at all, Anne. Mr. Rhodes is the one who's going to be hurting if he doesn't tell me where my daughter is located." She couldn't believe this was even up for debate.

"We all want Madison back." Brianna stepped forward, placing herself square in Tracy's line of sight. "But this isn't the way to do it."

"He knows where she is. I can get it out of him. All it takes is a little convincing." Tracy hoisted the three-inch-thick log up and knotted the first strip of cord to one end. "As soon as the first flame singes his skin, he'll talk."

"Mrs. Sloane, please, listen to what you're saying. You're going to kill him."

Tracy fixed her eyes on Peyton. "And so what if I do? He won't be the first man I've killed since the EMP hit. How many have we taken down? How many have we killed as a group? Don't you see? This is how it is now."

"It doesn't have to be."

She snorted. How many times had they had this conversation? "Yes, it does. If I don't do this, Madison will die. Whoever she's with will kill her and then they'll come for us. We need to get Madison back and eliminate the threat."

"For all you know, that man is bluffing and there isn't anyone else."

"I don't believe that."

Brianna interrupted the argument. "Let me search for her. I'm a good tracker. I can follow Hampton's trail in from the forest and go farther out. If Madison's out there somewhere, I can find her."

Anne agreed. "Brianna's as skilled a hunter as her father. She can find them."

"It'll be like searching for a needle in a haystack."

"No. It won't. We already canvassed the immediate area and they aren't there. That means they didn't just scout this place out. They have a camp. Most likely within a day's hike."

"You'll never find it."

"Give me a chance to try."

"We don't have that kind of time."

Brianna ran a hand through her hair. "Mrs. Sloane, please. Madison is my friend. I want her back, too."

"Then help me truss that man up on this log and light a fire. We'll get the answers."

Peyton interjected. "What if they don't know Hampton's missing? If you kill him before we get Madison back, they might never let her go."

Tracy paused. "What are you getting at?"

"We could make a trade. Hampton for Madison."

Anne agreed. "He's no good as a trade if he's dead."

Tracy frowned. The thought of letting Hampton go didn't sit well with her at all. She wanted Madison back and this man to suffer. But why? Because she was angry? Afraid? Sick of being bullied and attacked and taken advantage of?

She stared at the bunch of rope in her hand. If Walter were there, he would already have Madison back and these people, whoever they were, wouldn't be a threat. "What if this is just the beginning? What if they attack us?"

"Then we fight back."

Tracy didn't want to concede, not when her daughter was out there somewhere and the man tied up in the kitchen might know where.

Anne walked up to her and reached for her shoulder.

Kindness shone in her brown eyes. "What if we'd shot first when you arrived?"

"You wouldn't have. Brianna was with us."

"We could have turned you out and sent you on your way."

"We knew the risks and if that happened, we would have been okay."

Anne shook her head. "You can't rush to judgment, Tracy. Give these people a chance."

"It's a mistake."

"It's one I want to make. For us and our home." She motioned to Brianna. "Let Brianna scout the camp. She can find it and report back. Then we'll know what we're up against."

Brianna agreed. "We have a pair of walkie-talkies. They'll work over any range I can travel. As soon as I find them, I'll call you."

Tracy didn't like the idea one bit. All she could think of were the pitfalls. "What if you get hurt? Or they capture you and you can't talk?"

Brianna's brow knit as she thought it over. "I won't engage. I'll only scope them out. If they look dangerous, I'll call right away and tell you the location. You can mount a rescue that minute."

Tracy still preferred dragging the information out of Hampton. It could take Brianna days to find the camp. She settled on a middle way. "I'll hold off until tomorrow morning. If you don't find the camp and radio by eight tomorrow, I'm getting the information out of our prisoner. One way or another."

Brianna nodded. "Fair enough."

With a heavy heart, Tracy turned away from Brianna and her mother. It was well and good for the two of them to argue for leniency when it wasn't their flesh and blood on the line. Would they feel the same way if Madison were their family?

Peyton stopped beside her. "Brianna will find her faster than we can."

"I hope you're right, Peyton." She couldn't shake the feeling that her daughter was slipping away. Tracy twisted the rope in her hands. "I can't stand here and do nothing."

"You could help me patrol. Without Brianna, I'll have twice the ground to cover."

Tracy managed a small smile. "Thanks, Peyton. I will."

* * *

7:00 P.M.

TRACY STARED AT THE SLEEPING FORM OF THE MAN WHO walked onto the Clifton property and turned her whole world upside down. Ten hours had passed since Brianna disappeared out of sight in search of his camp.

Ten hours of radio silence. Tracy turned the radio around in her hands. If Brianna didn't call in soon with an update, she didn't know if she could wait until morning to find out what Hampton knew. He held the information in his head and she could get it out of him.

Would she still be the same woman when she

finished? Could she look her husband and daughter in the eye when they came home?

Tracy wasn't sure it mattered as long as Madison came home in one piece. She could sacrifice her own humanity for the life of her daughter. A metaphorical eye for an eye.

The moonlight cast long, jagged shadows across the floor of the kitchen. It lit the side of Hampton's face when he shifted on the chair. It would be so easy to end it right now.

He opened his eyes and focused on Tracy. "You're going to kill me, aren't you?"

"If I don't find my daughter, yes."

"Even if you do, why would you let me go?"

Tracy regarded him for a moment. An able-bodied man with the capacity for hard work. He could have made his own way. He didn't need to loot and steal. "You never should have walked onto this property."

"You have what we need."

"Who sent you?"

He sighed. "What does it matter?"

"If you tell me where they're holding my daughter, I'll let you live."

"And what if they don't have her? What if she's already dead?"

Tracy didn't respond. She reached for the cup of water sitting on the table and brought it toward Hampton's lips. "Drink. Can't have you dying of dehydration."

He guzzled the water, spilling half of it in his desperation. When the cup emptied, he sagged back against the wood slats of the chair. His head dipped low and at first Tracy thought he may have passed out. But then he lifted his head. "The camp is about a five-mile walk due north of here. It's at the nexus of a creek and an outcrop of rock."

Tracy didn't dare move a muscle. She inhaled and waited for him to continue.

"There's eleven people. The leader is Eileen. Used to be a pit boss in a mine in West Virginia. Only female to ever have the job. Only woman I ever saw who could bring a grown man to his knees with just a look."

He coughed a bit and Tracy rose to refill the cup. "How did all of you get together?"

"Eileen lived in the apartment complex where I worked. I was the maintenance guy. When all hell broke loose, she rounded a bunch of us up and we formed a little gang."

Tracy brought the cup back to Hampton. He drank a few more sips before turning away.

"At first we stayed in town, looting and stealing from the local places. But that all cleared out real quick. Eileen said we needed to find somewhere more long-term where we could make a life. Somewhere like this place."

"And what? Once you found it, you were just going to take it?"

He nodded.

"Why? You're capable. You could have made your own way."

"Eileen's been good to me." He snorted. "She's been good to all of us."

It didn't make sense. Why would able-bodied young people band together around a single woman?

Hampton smacked his lips again. "Did you search my pockets?"

She nodded.

"Find anything?"

"No."

"Damn." His body twitched. "I could really use a hit."

Tracy reeled. "Is that what Eileen has over you? Drugs?"

Hampton's leg jumped up and down. "She's old. She can get a million prescriptions with the snap of her fingers. Made her rich doling them all out, too. Doctors would rather give a complaining old lady pills than listen to her. Eileen turned it into a business."

Now it all made sense. Eileen turned her clients into a gang. With them reliant on her for their next high, she could ask them to do anything. Tracy frowned. At some point the woman's supplies had to run out. "What will you do when you run out of pills?"

Hampton chewed on his lip. "Eileen says we can make more. Just need a good base camp with a decent kitchen."

Tracy didn't know a lot about drugs, but she knew it took more than a kitchen in the woods. Even if they found the right equipment, Anne didn't stock the ingredients.

Was Eileen stringing them all along just to get what she wanted? What would happen when she did?

The radio in Tracy's hand crackled to life.

"I've found them. Over."

Tracy brought the radio up to her lips and held down the button. "They're drug addicts. Don't trust them."

"Don't worry. I'll bring Madison home."

"Brianna, wait! It's dangerous! Come back."

The radio went silent and Tracy waited for a response. It never came.

She glanced up at Hampton. She couldn't let Brianna walk into a camp of unstable addicts reliant on a single woman to save them. She stood up in a rush. "Don't fall asleep. We're leaving."

CHAPTER THIRTEEN

MADISON

Location Unknown
8:00 p.m.

Pain and singing. The two came together in a strange, swirling mix inside Madison's skull. She groaned and rolled her head, pausing as the dull ache shifted into sharp agony.

The singsong cadence picked up and the words filtered into Madison's consciousness.

Drove she ducklings to the water
Every morn just at nine,
Hit her foot against a splinter,
Fell into the foaming brine.

Ruby lips above the water,
   Blowing bubbles, soft and fine,
   But, alas, I was no swimmer,
   So I lost my Clementine.

She blinked and fought to focus despite the pain. Young voices of women, hushed and melodic, kept singing the morbid song she learned in grade school. Reds and oranges danced against the backdrop of darkness. Her lips were stuck together, caked in something thick and crusted.

Madison ran her tongue along the chapped edge and tasted the familiar tang of copper. *Blood.*

Blinking again, the world sharpened into discernible objects. A fire leaping and twisting in the night. Bodies huddled around it for warmth. Some small, some big.

A woman with white, wiry hair standing off to the side.

Madison licked again at the blood. It had to be her own. The front right side of her head screamed in agony and the same side of her face was stiff and thick. Had she fallen?

She thought back to what she remembered. Scouting in the forest. Sliding down the embankment. The rock. Hauling herself up.

Darkness.

Did she slip back down? Did someone rescue her? She tuned out the second round of the same folk song and concentrated. No, she didn't remember falling.

Crinkling her nose against an itch, Madison tried to

scratch it. Her arm didn't move more than an inch. She wiggled again. Her wrists were bound behind her, not too tightly, but secure enough to restrict her freedom.

She tasted her own blood again as memories flooded back. The man crumpled on the ground in front of her mother. The morning patrol.

Were these the rest of his crew?

The old woman across the fire stood still and proud, her long white braid stark against the darkness of her jacket. Wrinkles etched deep lines across her forehead and around her mouth, but she didn't seem delicate or weak.

There was nothing frail about her.

As Madison watched, a young boy of ten or twelve rushed up to her. The woman leaned over to listen before nodding. The boy scampered off. Was she the leader of this little group?

Madison heard movement behind her and shut her eyes.

"Is she still unconscious?"

Hands palmed her body and shook her by the shoulders. Madison let her head loll back and forth.

"Yeah. Lilly hit her good."

"You really think they'll give us the cabins when they find out we have this girl? She doesn't seem like much."

Madison wanted to protest, but she didn't dare move.

"I don't know. Eileen seems to think so."

"What about Hampton? Where is he?"

"That idiot couldn't find his way out of a paper bag.

He's probably lost in the forest. If he can't find the fire, then we'll go looking for him at first light."

"Eileen's not going to like it."

"She doesn't like anything. That old woman is meaner than a pit bull."

"And she holds on tighter, too. Have you felt her grip? She gave me a bruise on my arm that lasted a week."

Madison swallowed. If they were speaking of the white-haired woman, then Madison was thankful she didn't try to escape just now. A blow to the head was nothing compared to what could befall her if the whole group caught her running away. She needed to save her strength and wait for a better opportunity.

Whatever happened, Madison refused to let them take the cabins. The Clifton property would not fall to this gang of thugs in the woods. She would find a way to stop them.

"Did you find anything on patrol?"

"Naw. That hiker we found the other day was gone. Bastard drank all his beer before Otto found him."

"If we don't get into those cabins, we're gonna starve out here." The person talking snorted back a noseful of snot. Her voice lowered to just about a whisper. "And I need a hit somethin' fierce."

"Eileen promised. We get those cabins, we can get glassed all we want."

Madison swallowed. They wanted to take over the Clifton place to have a place to get high? Anger raged inside her, but Madison managed to stay still.

People came and went as the evening wore on,

emerging from the darkness to sit near the fire before disappearing again into the dark like apparitions. She counted eleven separate individuals. Five women including the white-haired leader, three men, and three kids ranging from barely out of diapers to a max of ten or twelve.

One kid caught her attention. A boy of nine or ten with a moppy head of hair always falling in his eyes. He skirted the fire and with each pass around the flames, his steps grew closer and closer to Madison's prone form. She needed someone to help her out of this mess. Would he be the one to do it?

As long as she lay still and kept her head canted into the dirt, the adults left her alone. But a boy with nothing to do was a curiosity magnet. He couldn't help himself.

He eased close enough that she could make out the swoosh on his Nikes and the fraying of his shoe laces. Dirt caked the hem of his jeans and stains streaked the denim. They had been out in the woods for a while.

Where were they from? What were they doing out there?

A cackle of a laugh rose up from near the fire and the boy jumped. He ran back toward the flames like he'd only been dancing, not stalking their prisoner.

Madison waited. She refused to let sleep or pain or impatience get the best of her. After the laughter died down and the adults resumed their hushed chats while watching the flames, the boy returned.

Could she risk it? She thought about the violence it took to bash the side of her head with a rock. Was that only the beginning?

As the boy came closer, she twitched. He froze, but didn't run. She twitched again, watching him through eyelids opened barely wide enough to see.

This time he glanced behind him before taking another step in her direction.

She fluttered her lashes. He stared. She focused on him. His eyes were wide and dark and unreadable. Did he fear her? Want to free her? Just pass the time?

Madison managed a small, painful smile.

He smiled back.

Maybe this will work. Maybe I'll get out of here. She opened her mouth to speak when the white-haired woman's commanding voice cut across the camp.

"David! You get away from the prisoner this instant! Stephanie, guard her!"

The boy shuddered and turned on his heel, running away and taking any hope of escape with him. A woman rose from her seat beside the fire and Madison shut her eyes.

Boots stomped up to the space between her knees and head and a toe nudged her middle. "When can we wake her up?"

"In the morning. If Hampton's not back by first light, we go to them." The woman's voice carried with gravelly weight. "Those cabins will be ours."

The old woman. She was the leader, Eileen. Madison swallowed. They were all in on it together. The man who showed up at the Cliftons' front door. These people in the woods. She had to get out of there and save her family. She had to warn them.

As the boots retreated, Madison risked a quick

glance. Stephanie took up position five feet away with her side facing Madison and her face warmed by the fire. Madison wriggled her hands behind her back. The straps holding her wrists together cut into her skin, but she braced against the pain.

There was give in the ties. If she worked hard and long enough, she might break loose. It was her only chance. No one was going to help her. She would have to help herself.

CHAPTER FOURTEEN

DANI

NORTHERN CALIFORNIA FOREST
   8:00 p.m.

THE CIRCLE OF LIGHT BARELY LIT THE GROUND IN FRONT
of Dani's feet. With only two flashlights and four people,
there wasn't enough to go around, but they couldn't
stop. Not with close to twenty miles between them and
the Clifton property and a potential killer in the woods.

As soon as Colt explained about the sleeping bag
and the blood all over the campsite, Walter picked up
the pace, marching through the woods like a robot who
never tired. Dani struggled to keep up. Her feet were
lead blocks, her back ached, and she could barely keep
her eyes open.

Another step and she stumbled, catching herself
with an outstretched hand. Lottie yipped at her heels,
encouraging her to keep going.

"You okay back there?" Colt's voice carried in the darkness.

"Yeah. Just tripped."

Larkin's voice sounded from the right. "Need a flashlight in the back?"

"No. You need to know what's coming." Dani tried to pick up the pace and keep closer to the men leading the charge.

The backpack straps cut into her skin and she slipped her thumbs beneath the thin padding to give her shoulders some relief. With her mind occupied by the pain and discomfort, she walked on autopilot, not scanning for latent danger. All she could think about was a bed and a blanket or even a soft spot on the ground to curl up and sleep.

The tree root hid beneath a pile of fallen leaves. Her left foot hooked it and caught. She tried to disentangle her hands from her pack, but everything happened so fast. She was upright and walking, then she was falling in the dark.

Her body slammed into the ground face-first and air fled her lungs. The backpack smothered her, pressing her chest into the dirt and leaves. Dani struggled to come free, but the pack proved too strong. Something wet and warm coated her face and filled her nose. She gagged.

Blood.

"H-Help!" Dani tried to call out, but her voice was too weak. She couldn't get enough air into her lungs to speak. Darkness surrounded her and a ringing sounded in her ears.

Something wet nosed her cheek and Dani twitched. A bark cut through the noise inside her skull. *Lottie*.

She was so tiny, but so strong.

All at once the weight pressing her into the ground lifted. Dani sucked in a breath of air.

"Walter! Bring the light. Quick!"

Colt's voice and warmth enveloped her. He found her.

She tried to speak. "Th-Th…"

"*Shh*. Don't move. You could have broken something."

A light flashed in her eyes and Dani slammed them shut. Men's voices rose and fell and she struggled to make sense of them.

"There's blood everywhere. Did she fall on a branch?"

"It's her head. There's a nasty gash."

Hands gripped her shoulders and with a grunt, someone rolled her over onto her back.

"Her leg is twisted. Could be broken."

"We've got to stop that bleeding. Get me a towel."

Something soft but heavy pressed down on the side of Dani's head.

"Easy there. Don't fight it. Can you hear me, Dani?"

She smacked her lips. When did they get so big? "Y-Yes." Her tongue filled up her mouth like a water balloon in a jar and she couldn't make it cooperate.

"Good. I'm going to move your leg. You tell me if it hurts."

Dani said something she hoped was close to "*Okay*."

Pain shot up her leg and she screamed.

"All right. If it's not broken, it's badly sprained."

The pressure stayed on her head, but Colt's voice retreated. She strained to listen. "We can't move her until the morning. There's no way she'll be able to walk and that gash on her head needs stitches."

"I don't have the equipment."

"We can use duct tape or fishing line. Anything to get it closed and stop the blood. Once we reach the cabins, we can fix it up for real."

Nausea threatened to bring her dinner of jerky and water back up her throat. Dani moaned.

"Easy. You've had quite a fall."

She struggled to sit up, but a hand pressed her back down. "Just take it slow. Don't sit up."

"Sick. I'm going——"

Hands hoisted her up from behind and Dani leaned against something solid and warm. "Just don't get it on my jacket, will you?"

Larkin. Always the one for humor. Dani smiled despite the pain and vertigo. "Ha, ha."

"At least I know your brain isn't as twisted as your leg."

"Says who?"

He chuckled and Dani blinked her eyes open. The dizziness retreated as she tried to bring the world into focus. The longer she sat upright without the weight of the pack stifling her breath or blood dripping into her eye, the more lucid she became.

After a few minutes, she glanced at Larkin. He still held the cloth tight to her head. In the dark, she couldn't see the blood, but she knew the fabric must be thick with it. She would never make it to the Cliftons' place like this.

She smacked her lips together again and cleared her throat. "You should get going."

Larkin shifted his position and brought his head down close enough to look in her eyes. "Maybe you hit your head harder than I thought."

"I mean it." Dani swallowed down a mix of spit and blood. "I'm going to slow you down."

"We aren't leaving you."

Leaves rustled and Colt crouched down beside her. "How are you?"

"I've been better. But I think I'm okay." Dani meant what she said. The longer she sat there, the more her wits came back. Her head pounded and her leg throbbed, but she could think and speak. "You need to get going. Get to the Cliftons' place and make sure everyone is safe."

"No. You can't walk. We're setting up camp for the night."

Dani reached out and clutched at Colt's arm. "No. I want you to leave me here. After you get Walter home, you can come back for me."

"Don't be ridiculous. We're doing no such thing."

"I'm stealing time he doesn't have."

Colt took over from Larkin, pressing his own hand on top of Dani's wound. "I am not leaving you, so stop arguing with me about it."

She stared up into his eyes and saw determination and fear staring back. "I'll be okay here, Colt. I can handle a few days in the woods."

"No."

"Walter is worried about his family."

"And I'm worried about you."

Dani ground her teeth together. This was why she didn't want to go with Walter. Now she'd gone and made his life difficult. Now she could end up getting someone else killed.

A flashlight beam bounced around the surrounding forest floor, highlighting ferns and twigs before coming to rest on Dani's injured leg. Walter crouched beside her and focused the light on her ankle.

"Is it broken?"

"I don't think so." She straightened her leg out a bit and lifted it in the air. "I think it would hurt more."

"Good." He brought the flashlight up toward her face and Dani shut her eyes. "Let's take a look at your head."

The pressure eased on her scalp and Dani gasped against the sudden rush of pain.

No one said anything.

"That good, huh?"

Walter lowered the flashlight and the pressure came back even harder than before. Dani opened her eyes.

"You've got a nasty gash that needs to be cleaned and closed somehow. It won't be pleasant."

Dani nodded a fraction. "Whatever you have to do, just do it."

Walter stood up. "I'll start a fire. We'll need to boil some water."

The flashlight beam bounded off and Dani exhaled. "I'm sorry I've screwed everything up."

"Don't apologize. We're all exhausted. A night's rest will do us all good."

Dani didn't say any more. She watched the flashlight wander around the vicinity, dropping to a low little circle when Walter bent to gather wood and tinder, expanding when he walked. After a few minutes, it clicked off.

Her pupils swelled as she took in the night. Darkness all around. Leaves from the tree canopy above them obscured most of the moonlight. It was eerie in the forest without light. Anyone could be lurking just out of reach.

She glanced to her right and froze. *What is that?* A little orb of light bounced and weaved and flickered in the distance. She couldn't tell how close or how far away, only that it was moving. Someone else was in the forest.

Dani reached for Colt's arm and squeezed. "Colt."

He shushed her. "I see it." He reached for her hand, fumbling about in the dark. "Grab the rag. Hold it tight on your head."

She did as she was told, pressing her hand against the wound as he stood up.

Hushed male voices echoed around her, but she couldn't make out the words.

Larkin's whisper made her jump. "Colt and Walter are going to check it out."

"You should go, too."

"We're not leaving you alone."

Dani protested. "I have Lottie. She'll bark if anyone comes near."

"That's ridiculous."

Dani refused to back down. "You have no idea what you're up against. Go. I'll be fine."

Larkin hesitated for a moment before placing two cold objects in her hands. A gun and a flashlight. "Only for emergencies. Otherwise stay quiet and dark."

"Be careful."

"Always." The sound of his footsteps retreated and Dani was alone.

She strained to listen, but the sounds of the forest eclipsed any footsteps. Colt, Walter, and Larkin were out there, somewhere.

So was someone else.

Dani slipped her fingers around the cold grip of the gun. The light in the distance was gone.

CHAPTER FIFTEEN

MADISON

Location Unknown
  10:00 p.m.

Blood coated Madison's wrists and slicked the plastic as it cut deeper into her skin. Over the course of the last two hours, Madison worked on the zip ties, rubbing and twisting her wrists back and forth as she stretched the plastic a fraction at a time.

She would either rub all the skin off her wrists or the plastic would stretch enough to free her hands. Maybe both.

As she worked the ties, Madison glanced around, careful not to move more than necessary. All quiet. Embers glowed where the fire raged earlier that night. Only one sentry remained awake: a woman with a ratty brown ponytail and a rifle she didn't seem comfortable holding. If Madison could free herself, now was the best time. She could overpower a novice with a gun.

Even the white-haired woman was gone. She had visited Madison once that night, pushing back her matted hair and propping open one of her eyelids. Madison pretended to be unconscious and hung in the woman's hand like a marionette with no puppet master. It seemed to satisfy the old woman, but Madison knew that come morning anything could happen.

If she were still there when the sun rose, then she might never escape. Her family wouldn't know these horrible people were coming to attack. The Cliftons would suffer.

Madison picked up the pace, hyped up on adrenaline and hunger. If only she could move more than her wrists, but she couldn't risk catching the sentry's attention until she broke free.

As the woman turned her way, Madison closed her eyes and went limp. She counted to one hundred and peeled one eye open. The sentry was gone.

Where is she?

Madison risked discovery, opening both eyes and squinting into the dark. A lumpy shape seemed to huddle in near the fire. Had the woman sat down? Bundled herself in a blanket?

It didn't make sense. Madison eased forward as quietly as possible, using the toe of her boot as leverage to propel her body forward. The closer she inched, the more she could see. No blanket, so sack of potatoes.

The sentry lay in a heap on the ground, not moving.

Fear spiked Madison's pulse and she swiveled

around. Was the camp under attack? She scanned the dark for signs of interlopers. Her mother had to know she was missing by now. Could she be there, trying to save her?

A thump sounded behind her and Madison froze. She would be a sitting duck with restrained hands and feet and no weapon.

Fight or flight warred inside the four chambers of her heart. Fighting alongside whoever came to tear these people apart would bring satisfaction and justice. But if they weren't friendly, it could get her killed. She needed to run.

If only her ankles weren't strapped together.

Madison rolled forward and rose up onto her knees. Working her way around in a full circle, she took stock. The sentry still lay on the ground. Blobs of tents and tarps and the structures these people called home dotted the perimeter.

No movement.

A rustle behind her.

Madison spun on her knees and came face to face with a sight that stole her breath. "Brianna!"

"Hush or you'll wake them up." Her former college roommate rushed toward her.

The blade of knife caught the moonlight and Madison turned to give Brianna access to her hands. It took a few saws of the blade, but relief flooded Madison's shoulders and wrists when the zip ties snapped. Brianna made fast work of the one around her ankles as well.

I'm free. She stared at the bloody mess of her wrists.

"Are you all right?"

Madison nodded.

"Good. We need to move."

Madison grabbed Brianna's arm. "They're going to attack us."

"I know. We need to get home and warn the others." Brianna rose up to stand but Madison didn't follow.

She thought about their options and the urge to fight filled her once more. "We could end it right now. Kill them while they sleep."

Brianna paused. "How many are there?"

"Eleven. Three are kids."

"We can't take them all."

"We could go for their leader. She's an older woman. White hair."

Brianna chewed on her lip. "Where is she?"

Madison stood up and a pang of dizziness threatened to throw her to the ground. She reached for Brianna to keep her up. "I don't know. I was unconscious most of the day. I didn't come to until it was dark."

"We can't risk it. By the time we find her, someone will be awake." She pulled on Madison's sleeve. "Let's go."

Madison knew Brianna was right, but the thought of leaving Eileen alive tore at her insides. She would be mounting an attack on the Cliftons' place as soon as the sun rose. How could they leave her to do it?

The sentry on the ground moaned and Brianna tugged harder on Madison's arm. "We're leaving. Now."

Brianna dragged Madison away from the camp and

into the cover of the woods. A hundred yards from the fire, she pulled her arm free. "How far away are we?"

"About five miles, give or take. There's a gulley in between, but no other natural defenses."

"Would we have seen them coming if they attacked?"

Brianna shook her head. "Not from this direction."

Everything Madison feared was coming true. There were no safe spaces anymore. No places she could let her guard down and just live. Was all of that a fantasy constructed by light bulbs and alarm systems? Was anywhere truly safe before the grid failed, or were people always this ruthless?

A shout sounded back at the camp and Brianna grabbed her arm. "Run!"

Together they bounded into the forest, using the little moonlight that filtered through the trees to see. Flashlights clicked on in the distance behind them, bouncing little orbs of light in every direction.

"If they catch us, we're toast." Brianna picked up the pace and Madison struggled to keep up.

Leaves and branches slapped her in the face and rocks and roots tripped up her feet. She stumbled again and again, barely staying upright as she ran. Her head pounded from the beating she took that morning and her vision dimmed.

Shouts behind them grew louder and more desperate. Madison wasn't sure she could run five miles. She wasn't sure she could run another step. The forest went on forever. Over and over, her feet thudded on the ground, every step closer to their destination.

Home. I'm trying to go home. Visions of Sacramento and the little house her parents used to own filled her mind, followed by flames and gunshots and ashes and soot. Home was gone. Madison would never see it again.

"Brianna, I—" It was Brianna's home they needed to find; the Clifton cabin. Their mothers and Peyton and the future.

Madison staggered and leaves rose up to meet her. Cold air battered her face. Twigs scratched her hands.

"Keep going. We can't stop!" Brianna's voice cut through the fog and Madison dragged herself out of the dirt. She tried to follow, but the pounding in her head only grew louder and louder until all she could hear was the relentless rhythm. Her legs wobbled and knees sank again. Her fingers pierced the forest floor, diving beneath the leaves to the soft earth.

"Brianna..." Her shout came out in a whisper. Her body sagged toward the ground. She couldn't go on. The pain in her head threatened to drive her mad. *How could anyone live like this?*

"Madison!" Hands reached under her arms and tried to haul her up by the armpits. She sagged against the struggle.

"Madison, get up! They're coming." Brianna tugged on her again. "We can hide, but you have to move!"

The fear in Brianna's voice broke through the confusion and Madison struggled to stand. Brianna looped an arm around her middle and half-walked, half-carried her forward.

Time slowed. The night grew darker while flashes of color swam in front of her eyes. "I'm going to pass out."

"Just hold on."

The dirt loomed up again, but this time Madison didn't fall into it. Instead, Brianna eased her toward the ground. Her back wedged against a rock. Leaves whipped her face.

"Stay low. Pull your jacket over your head." Rustling sounded beside her and Brianna's voice carried from what seemed like miles away. "If we're quiet they might miss us."

Madison couldn't even respond. Her tongue filled her mouth and cotton packed the space between her ears. Lights danced and bobbed in front of her and she couldn't tell if they were part of her imagination or the members of the camp coming to haul them back.

The rock and ground pressed in around her. Darkness washed over her as she closed her eyes.

Some part of her knew it was wrong to sleep, but the rest of her body screamed for relief. Whatever strength she'd possessed back at the camp was left behind in footprints and drops of blood. The side of her head throbbed.

Cold seeped beneath her jacket and down her sleeves. She shivered in semi-consciousness, barely aware of voices and lights and the trembling body lying next to her.

Brianna? Madison's thoughts slowed to sludge. She couldn't feel her fingers or her toes or figure out how to say a single word. Exhaustion and pain overcame her. Staying awake was pointless when she couldn't even feel her face.

CHAPTER SIXTEEN

DANI

Northern California Forest
   10:00 p.m.

Lottie crouched in Dani's lap, small and trembling. If it weren't for the heat the little dog radiated, Dani would have thought the shivers were her own. The longer she sat in the dark, the more terrifying it became.

The absence of light turned an ordinary forest into a sinister playground of imaginary ghouls and goblins. Every snap of a twig or rustle of leaves was the boogeyman coming to claim Dani as a victim.

She was never afraid of nighttime in the city. The steady glow of electricity made even the darkest back alley gray and mostly visible. She could skirt the light and stay safe in the shadows.

But the darkness of the forest clung to her skin and

chilled her bones. Colt, Larkin, and Walter had experience in the total blackness. How many missions had Colt gone on where sight was the least of his abilities? Dani was sure the three of them had spent more than one night fighting an unseen enemy.

Not her. Every bad guy she'd ever encountered, from her mother to a drug dealer to Colonel Jarvis, attacked in the light.

The wound on her head still oozed, the smell of her blood cloying in the stillness. Dani kept the rag pressed against her scalp. Sooner or later it would either stop bleeding or she would pass out. She almost hoped for the latter.

The night dragged on. No light. No sounds of men returning from an expedition. No reassuring voices or glimpse of sunrise. It could have been minutes or hours, Dani had no idea. She struggled to stay awake, each blink drawing out longer and longer until her eyes closed longer than they managed to stay open.

* * *

Dani jerked upright.

Did I fall asleep? Pass out? Her hand with the rag lay limp in her lap. Lottie wasn't there; the little spot the dog warmed was cold and empty.

Darkness still stretched on and on in front of her, broken only by tricks of her imagination. She brought her fingers up and gingerly probed her head. The gash stopped bleeding at some point in the night, but blood matted her hair and covered her shirt and turned her into a nasty, injured mess.

Her ankle still throbbed and as Dani attempted to move it, pain shot up her leg. She reached out for the gun and flashlight, fingers stumbling over them a foot away from where she sat. *Yes*. At least she still had a weapon.

With a scratchy throat, she called for the dog in a hoarse whisper. "Lottie! Lottie! Come here, girl."

Silence.

She frowned and picked up the flashlight. *Should I use it?* She thought about Colt out in the dark somewhere, hunting for the source of the light. If they could see someone from a mile away, anyone out there could see her.

A shiver ran through her. The temperature had dropped. Cold seeped through Dani's clothes. She needed a fire or needed to move. *Soon*.

"Lottie! Lottie, come!"

Still no dog. Where was she? It wasn't like Lottie to run off. When someone was hurt or needed help, the little dog was always right there, ready and able.

A noise startled her and Dani sat in the stillness and listened. It came again, low and rumbling. A growl.

Is that Lottie? She strained to hear.

Leaves rustled.

Fur scraped the back of her hand. Dani stifled a scream.

"Lottie!" The little dog clambered up into Dani's lap. "You're safe!"

The dog whined and licked Dani's palm.

"What is it, girl? What's wrong?"

Dani didn't have time to figure it out. A noise sounded again. More like a snort or a snuffle.

It didn't come from the Yorkie in her lap.

Scooping up Lottie, Dani held her close while she fumbled with the flashlight. *Should I use it? Should I wait?*

If Lottie would stay quiet, maybe whatever was out there would go away.

A scuffle in the distance. Another huffing snort. This time closer. Louder.

Whatever was out there, it wasn't leaving. Dani rooted around on the ground until her fingers tumbled over a rock. She picked it up and threw it as hard as possible toward the noise.

Dani didn't know much about wild animals. What could it be? A coyote? She remembered reading once about a mountain lion that plagued Lake Tahoe, killing people's pets in their backyards. Could a big cat be prowling the night, looking for a tasty morsel like Lottie to eat?

The little dog growled again and the animal in the woods answered. Dani pressed her lips together. She could always turn on the flashlight, but what good would it do?

The animal would see her. So would everyone else. Where was Colt? She opened her mouth to shout for him, but closed it just as fast.

Could it be a person? Could the noise be someone's dog on a leash?

The possibilities were endless. All Dani could do was wait.

She eased Lottie's little trembling body down onto her lap and reached for the flashlight. With the gun in one hand and the flashlight in the other, Dani waited.

One finger rested on the trigger and one on the button of the light. She could face whatever was out there. Coyote, dog, or snarling cat.

Leaves rustled no more than ten feet away. There was a rooting sound, like whatever it was needed to smell its way toward her. Dani's heart thundered in her chest like a stampede of wild horses. She brought the flashlight up, held it out in front of her.

Whatever was out there, she had to know. The noise came closer. Lottie shifted on Dani's lap, her little claws digging into Dani's thighs as she snarled.

That's it. No more waiting. I have to know.

Dani pushed the button and flooded the immediate vicinity in light.

All she saw was fur. Dark, shaggy fur, black goggling eyes, and an enormous paw.

Oh my God.

It wasn't a coyote, or a man with a dog, or even a ferocious big cat.

The furry, snarling beast in front of her was a black bear.

A low, throaty noise sounded from deep within the bear's chest, almost like a hoot. It pulsed in and out and Dani shrank back in fear. The animal was massive. More than twice her size, it had to outweigh her by a hundred pounds at least.

Dani glanced at the handgun in her palm. Would it stop a bear?

The beast prowled in front of her, pacing back and forth and pawing at the ground. Dani kept the flashlight trained on its face, willing it to run away and leave her alone.

Lottie growled at the bear and it snarled back. *Oh, no.*

Dani raised the gun and pointed it at the bear's chest. "Go away! Shoo!"

The bear didn't listen. Missing fur and jagged scars marked the animal's chest. A fighter. A survivor. Dani didn't want to hurt it, but she wouldn't let it kill her.

She screamed louder. "Get out of here!"

The bear huffed and rose up on its hind legs, stretching to an impossible height. Dani stared in horror as it charged.

Ten feet, then five, then three. Dani screamed and shouted as Lottie scrambled off her lap to attack. "No! Lottie!"

She pulled the trigger on the gun and the shot pierced the forest, echoing along the ridges of the foothills. The bear didn't slow down.

A paw swiped. Lottie yipped. Dani fired again. "Fight me, not her, you bastard!"

The animal turned on Dani. Ferocious and wild with snarling teeth and massive claws as long as Dani's entire hand. It bounded toward her and Dani fired again.

Claws raked her arm and Dani screamed.

The flashlight flew from her grip and landed in the dirt. The forest plunged into darkness. She fired another shot as fur and spit and menace landed hard on top of her. The barrel of the handgun disappeared into a sea of matted, stinking fur.

Dani protected her face with her injured arm and pulled the trigger again and again until the magazine emptied.

The bear slumped on top of her, breath sawing out of its lungs and heating her face. As the life leaked from its bullet-riddled body, the full weight of the animal came to bear upon Dani's chest. Heavier than a linebacker, it pressed her into the dirt.

Dani scrabbled on the ground, searching for purchase to pull herself free. She would trade falling face-first with a heavy backpack for this any day of the week. Her lungs burned from lack of oxygen. Her eyes watered.

She gasped like a fish on a dock.

There had to be a way. She couldn't suffocate to death like this. Liquid ran into her eyes and Dani blinked it back. It trickled into her mouth and Dani tasted blood. The wound on her head was open and bleeding.

With the last of her energy, Dani pushed against the bear's chest. Spots of color swam before her eyes. The ringing in her ears picked back up.

Her fingers grew weak and discombobulated. Her head grew heavier and heavier. It was no use. She couldn't escape its weight or fur or the stench of defeat.

At last, Dani dropped her arms. They flopped on the ground beside her. She couldn't move the dead weight pressing her into the earth.

Dani closed her eyes and let pain and fear engulf her. *At least I'm not cold.*

She smiled to herself as flicks of light flitted across her eyelids. Voices filtered through the haze, but Dani couldn't understand them.

It was too late and she was tired. It was time to sleep.

CHAPTER SEVENTEEN

COLT

NORTHERN CALIFORNIA FOREST
11:00 p.m.

THE DAMN LIGHTS DISAPPEARED INTO THE FOREST without a trace. Colt had been up and down the stretch of land that bordered a ravine for over an hour with no luck. If it weren't for the moon directly overhead, he'd have fallen to his death a million times.

There was no way whoever was out there could just scramble down the ledge and across the stream below him. He didn't hallucinate the lights. None of them did. So where the hell were they?

As he stood there, fuming over what to do, a sound caught his ear. The noise echoed around the gulley, bouncing off the opposite bank and back. *Was that a gunshot?*

He had to get back to Dani. It had been way too

long and they'd wasted too much energy tracking a ghost. In the morning, they would have to hike out of there and Dani might not be able to walk. That ankle of hers was already swelling before he'd even left.

Another pop, followed by another and another. A whole series of them.

If only he could be sure what direction they came from. They could have been firecrackers or bullets, he couldn't tell, and thanks to the chasm next to him, Colt couldn't even be sure they weren't echoes of a single noise.

He turned away from the ravine and hustled back toward Dani's spot in the forest. At least Larkin was there to protect her.

Thanks to years of land navigation, he could make it back even without the moon as a guide. Hopefully Larkin had kept her warm and comfortable. She needed to recuperate before trekking the rest of the way to the cabin.

As Colt neared the area, he let out a short, low whistle. No one responded. Not Dani, nor Larkin, nor little Lottie. *Strange.* He tried again with two bursts at a higher pitch. Still nothing.

Colt slowed and readied his Sig. "Larkin!" he whisper-shouted into the trees.

Not a sound.

The hair on Colt's neck rose and he circled the makeshift camp, coming at it from the north instead of the south. His nostrils twitched as he caught the whiff of something musky and wild. An animal? He approached with caution, squinting as the shape of something large and humped loomed ahead.

Is that fur? He eased closer, breathing in the scent of dirty, wet fur and… is that blood? Colt rushed forward and the shape materialized out of the darkness.

What the…? A black bear's body lay stretched out, head to the side and mouth gaping. One paw stretched forward, claws dug halfway into the earth. Colt lowered into a crouch. *What's a bear doing at camp? Where's Dani or Larkin? Lottie should be barking or pawing at my feet.*

Colt poked at it with his gun and the ground shifted beneath it. A hint of something pale caught the light. Colt leaned closer and shoved at the bear's leg.

A familiar sweatshirt. A limp hand. *Oh, no.*

Colt stood up in a rush, shaking his head in disbelief. "Dani! Dani, can you hear me?"

Backing up a handful of steps, Colt charged like a linebacker about to topple an offensive line, dropping his shoulder as he slammed into the bear's side. The animal's carcass wobbled, but didn't move. He backed up and tried again.

He managed to rock the bear's dead weight up and off the ground. Dani's shoulder came into view. Blood soaked the front of her clothes. Colt grunted in rage and kept pushing. Drawing deep into his stores of adrenaline and fury, he shoved the animal with all his might until at last it flipped over onto its back.

Leaves and dirt puffed into the air as the bear's body landed beside Dani's.

Colt fell to his knees beside her. *Please be alive. Please.* Reaching for her neck, he searched for a pulse. *Come on.*

Come on. There! A faint thump, followed by another and another. They were weak and far apart, but her heart still beat. She hadn't left him.

Footfalls sounded behind him and Colt whirled around, gun drawn and ready.

Larkin emerged from the trees and stumbled to a stop. He lifted his hands. "It's just me, Colt. Put the gun down."

"How could you?" Colt kept the gun trained squarely on Larkin's chest. "You were supposed to stay."

Larkin frowned. "What are you talking about?" He craned his neck to the side, trying to see around Colt. "What the hell is that, a bear?"

"You left her here all by herself."

"She told me to. I gave her my flashlight and a gun. What's wrong? Where's Dani?"

Colt shuddered as anger flowed through his veins. "The bear attacked her. I found her almost crushed to death beneath it. She's unconscious."

"You can't be serious." Larkin shook his head in disbelief. "The bears around here don't attack people."

Colt thrust his hand in the bear's direction. "This one did. She's barely alive. There's blood everywhere. You did this. It's your fault."

Larkin opened his mouth and it hung there, gaping. After a moment, he sagged down to the ground to come eye-to-eye with Colt. "I'm sorry, Colt. I thought… Dani asked me to go. She was worried about you. I would never have left her if I knew… She said she had Lottie and a gun and begged me to go." He trailed off, his words choppy and choked with emotion.

"What the hell is going on?" Walter emerged from the darkness. He stopped at the sight. "Colt?"

Colt kept the gun pointed at Larkin. "He was supposed to stay."

Walter took a step forward. "Lower the gun."

"She's going to die and I wasn't here to stop it."

"What are you talking about?"

"See for yourself."

Walter clicked on a flashlight and panned the beam across the dead bear and Dani's limp form. She looked like a body on a mortician's slab, cold and lifeless. The flashlight clicked off. "Is she breathing?"

"Her heart's beating."

"Then we can't waste any more time. She needs medical attention and fast."

Colt snorted. "We're in the middle of nowhere."

"The cabin is ten miles. If we hurry we can get there by morning."

"We can't move her. Who knows what's broken."

Larkin spoke up. "One of us could leave now. If we jog, we could make it in a couple hours." He glanced up at Walter. "You said there's a Jeep, right?"

Walter nodded. "Larkin's right. We can get the Jeep and get back here faster than we can carry her."

"If you show me how to get there, I can go."

"No." Colt shook his head at Larkin. "You're not leaving my sight."

Walter knelt beside his pack and unzipped the top. "I'll go. It'll be faster that way." He fished out his canteen, a ration of jerky, and an extra magazine for the rifle slung across his back. "If I'm not back in three hours, start walking."

He eased closer to Colt and clicked on the flashlight once more. With a stick, Walter drew a map, pointing out all the landmarks between their current location and the cabin. "The cabin is due south, about ten miles. Skirt the gulley for the first two or three miles before it veers off to the east. Then it's a straight shot. The terrain slopes the whole way. We're on a grade."

Colt hoped like hell he wouldn't need to carry Dani the entire way. He scowled at Larkin again before lowering the gun. They would fight about it later. Right now, he needed to tend to Dani's obvious wounds.

Walter stood and clicked off the light. "I'll hurry."

"Thank you." Colt waited until he could no longer hear Walter's footsteps to turn his attention to Dani.

"I'll look around on the ground for the flashlight I left with her." Larkin stood as he spoke. "You'll need it to clean her up."

Colt ground his teeth together. The last thing he wanted was to accept help from the man responsible, but he had no choice. Dani had been through so much in her short fifteen years. She didn't deserve to die ten miles from a place she might be able to call home. He refused to think about Lottie and what must have befallen her.

A light clicked on ten feet away and Larkin hustled up with the flashlight. "She must have lost it in the struggle."

Colt took it without a word. Starting with her feet, he used the light to inspect Dani's body. Her twisted ankle was swollen, but otherwise fine. By the time she regained enough strength to walk, it should be healed.

The rest of her was another story. Blood covered her shirt and jeans, so thick in places, it dried into blobby pools. Colt cursed under his breath. How was she still alive? There had to be enough blood for three people.

Larkin whistled from the other side of the bear and Colt jerked his head up. "What is it?"

"Shine the light over here, will you?"

Colt frowned, but obliged, panning the flashlight beam across the bear carcass.

"There's enough bullet holes in this bear to stop an army. Dani must have fired every round into its chest."

Colt leaned over her body to get a closer look. Larkin was right; bloody holes pocked the entire front of the oversized beast. Colt brought the light back to Dani's body. Maybe all the blood wasn't her own.

Maybe most of it belonged to the bear she took down all on her own. He reached with tentative fingers for the hem of her shirt and lifted it up enough to see underneath. No oozing wounds. No gaping slash marks.

Colt exhaled in relief. *She might be okay.* He glanced up at Larkin. "Get some water and a rag, will you? We need to clean her up."

As Larkin made his way to the packs, Colt closed his eyes. In a few hours, they would be inside a cabin with heat and light and medical equipment. Even if Dani broke a few ribs or an arm, they could treat her. Colt had faith that she would survive. He couldn't count on anything else.

DAY FORTY-FIVE

CHAPTER EIGHTEEN

TRACY

Northern California Forest

12:00 a.m.

Hampton stumbled and Tracy hauled him up by the rope lashing his wrists together. "Next time, I won't pick you up. Your face can lead the way instead of your feet."

The man muttered under his breath and Tracy tugged him extra hard. "Which way now?"

"If you stopped jerking me around for more than a minute, maybe I could tell you."

With an exhale full of impatience, Tracy stopped and turned to face her prisoner. "Do I need to remind you that you're the one who ambushed us? You're the one who wanted to take what doesn't belong to you."

He scowled. "All of you have more than enough. Why can't you share?"

"We worked for everything we have. People died for

some of our supplies. And you want us to what, hand them over?"

"It's not our fault we didn't have anything."

Tracy raised an eyebrow. "It isn't?"

Hampton shook his head. "You try living off a janitor's pay and see how far it gets you."

She stared at his clothes and his hollow cheeks. "Drugs can't help."

He wiped his nose on his shoulder. "They pass the time."

"Books pass the time. Drugs just ruin your life." She shuddered as childhood memories rose to the surface. Her mother had been a user. Look how that turned out.

"Never been much of a reader."

I was a librarian.

Hampton brought his tied hands up to his face and chewed on a thumbnail. If Eileen was keeping her little group together with some pills as favors, then Hampton was crashing hard. Thirteen hours was a long time to go without a hit.

If she wanted him to lead her to the camp, they needed to get on with it. "Enough chitchat. Let's get going." She tugged on the rope and pulled his hands away from his face.

He motioned with his head. "It's that way."

They walked on in silence with nothing but the moon as their guide. When the trees closed in and the forest darkened too much to see, Tracy navigated to a thinner patch while maintaining the same general direction. It had been hours since Brianna radioed and still they hadn't come across the camp.

She glanced back at Hampton. Was he pointing her in the right direction? Did he even know what way to go?

They could be lost out in the woods, veering so far off course it would take days to make it back. Tracy slowed. "Any landmarks I should be looking for?"

Hampton scratched at the scabs forming on his chin. "There's a creek past the camp with a real big drop off on either side. Steph almost fell in it on the way."

"What about on this side?"

He shook his head. "Nope. Nothin'."

Great. Tracy exhaled and kept walking, keeping the moon in her sights as a general guide. After another half hour, they came upon an outcropping of rock and she stopped to assess.

Even walking at the two miles an hour they were managing, the camp should be near. Heck, she should be on top of it. Either they were slower than she anticipated, or Hampton directed her off the mark.

She turned to him. "Are you sure we're going the right way?"

He shrugged. "I don't know. It all looks the same in the dark."

Tracy cursed. She should kill him and eliminate the dead weight. Instead, she leaned against the boulder and closed her eyes. What a fool she'd been, thinking she could come out here without a plan and rescue Brianna. If her luck kept up, Brianna would need to rescue her.

"Mrs. Sloane? Is that you?"

Now I'm hallucinating. Wonderful. Tracy opened her

eyes. Brianna Clifton stood no more than two feet in front of her, gun drawn and ready.

"Brianna?"

The girl shushed her and stepped closer. Her voice barely carried to Tracy's ear. "What are you doing here?"

"I came to find you. Those people are dangerous."

"I know." Brianna glanced at Hampton with a wary eye. "I got Madison and we escaped, but they're looking for us."

Tracy swallowed. "Madison's alive?"

Brianna nodded. "The camp is about a mile ahead. We made it this far before we had to take cover."

Looking past the twenty-year-old, Tracy scoured the dark for her daughter. She wasn't there. Her heart leapt in her chest. "Where's Madison?"

Brianna hesitated. The moonlight glanced off her teeth as she nibbled on her lip. "She's nearby, but hurt. I can't move her on my own."

Both women focused on Hampton. Now he wasn't just a loose cannon, but a liability. They couldn't handle him and an injured Madison. But they couldn't cut him loose, either.

Tracy would have to kill him. She reached for the rifle on her shoulder, but paused halfway. A gunshot would be too loud.

Hampton began to fidget, bouncing back and forth on his feet as if he knew what was coming. "You can just let me go. I won't tell."

"He can't be trusted."

Tracy nodded. "I know." She didn't want to kill a

man with her bare hands. How would she even do it? Bash his head in? Choke him? It was one thing to pull a trigger or fight for her life in the heat of the moment. But to kill a man in cold blood without making a sound? It wasn't in her.

Brianna motioned to the nearest tree. "We can tie him up. Gag him."

"It's a risk."

"Hey! Don't I get a say here?" Hampton yanked on the rope. It slid along Tracy's palm. *Damn it.* Now she didn't have a choice. She wrapped the excess around her hand and pulled hard.

Hampton stumbled toward her. Before he could shout and alert anyone to his presence, she grabbed the hem of her T-shirt and yanked. The soft fabric tore and Tracy bunched up the strip.

Backpedaling away from her, Hampton put up his tied hands in defense. He opened his mouth to scream and Tracy shoved the wad of cotton inside. He tried to shout or spit it out, but Tracy held his mouth shut with her hand.

"Cut some of the rope and tie it around his mouth."

Brianna pulled a knife from her boot and did as Tracy instructed. Looping the rope around the rag stuffed in Hampton's mouth, Brianna tied it behind his head.

He tried to scream, but the sound came out muffled and weak. It could have been an animal in the woods or a bird in the air. Nothing to raise suspicions.

Tracy dragged him over to the nearest tree and tied the remaining rope around the trunk. She patted him on the shoulder. "Be thankful I'm not putting a bullet between your eyes."

He cursed at her with wide eyes and a shake of his head.

"When you get out of this, stop using and get clean. Then go find a library and get yourself some books. You can learn all sorts of things. Like how to survive."

She stepped away and Brianna grabbed her by the arm. "Madison is this way. We should hurry."

Tracy followed Brianna to a spot just on the other side of the rock she'd leaned up against to rest. At the base of the boulder, Brianna brushed away leaves and fallen branches to reveal Tracy's daughter.

Oh, honey. Tracy fell to her knees and reached for Madison. A clump of matted hair turned rusted brown from blood covered the side of her face. "Is she hurt badly?"

"I don't know. She has a bad cut on her head and I think a concussion. She collapsed while we were running and hasn't come to since."

Tracy nodded. They needed to get her to safety as soon as possible. Then they could decide what to do about Eileen and the rest of her tribe.

With gentle hands, Tracy lifted her daughter. Brianna slipped one shoulder under Madison's left side and Tracy took the right. Together they began the slow, agonizing trek back to the Clifton compound.

As soon as Madison stabilized, Tracy would gather the necessary weapons and come up with a plan. These people who wanted what they didn't earn would not destroy the Cliftons' property. They wouldn't be the end of the hope that bloomed inside her daughter's chest.

Madison would wake up to safety and sunshine and a future as bright as any sunny day. They would not have to start again somewhere new.

This time, Tracy wouldn't sit back and let the fight come to her. She would confront it head-on. No prisoners. No leniency. She would defend her daughter until her last breath.

CHAPTER NINETEEN
WALTER

NORTHERN CALIFORNIA FOREST

12:30 a.m.

DAMN FOREST. WALTER HAD SPENT HIS FAIR SHARE OF time land nav'ing in forests up and down the eastern seaboard, but he thought he'd left that all behind twenty years ago. Now here he was, forty-five years old, double-timing it through trees and ferns and blackberry bushes.

This wasn't the way he'd hoped to spend his retirement. Not that he could call struggling to survive in lawless anarchy retirement, but he wouldn't exactly be taking to the skies for a commercial airline any time soon.

By his estimates, he was nearing the halfway point. Too damn slow. One look at Dani's pale cheeks and limp fingers and Walter knew they were on borrowed time. The girl might already be dead.

Adjusting his rifle, he loped into a thinner stand of trees. The moon shone bright and full above him and he stopped for a drink of water. As the pounding of his heart slowed and he stopped slurping, the sounds of harsh words caught his ear.

"—be so stupid."

"I swear, she had to have help."

"Nonsense. How could they find us up here? It's the middle of the damn night."

"I was watching her the whole time. Someone else hit me!"

"Harder than this?"

The smack of skin on skin echoed through the forest and Walter dropped to a crouch. He didn't recognize the voices. Not Anne nor Tracy nor any of the kids. These were strangers. He crept forward on silent feet, rolling his steps to minimize the sound.

Were they the same people who tore up the camp a few miles back? Walter thought about the sleeping bag covered in blood and empty beer cans. If they were involved, then he needed to be wary.

"Eileen, please. I'm telling the truth." The younger voice turned pleading. A woman, not much older than Madison by the sound of her.

Walter eased behind a tree as the faint glow of a dying fire came into view. *Damn*. Not what he'd hoped for. In front of him sat a makeshift little camp.

From his vantage point, he counted five structures: two tents, a tarp slung over a rope, and two other pale manmade forms that must have been improvised sleeping quarters. Sheets strung on a line? Blankets? It didn't matter.

These were not the markings of seasoned backpackers. City dwellers had infiltrated the forest. Two women stood in the middle, their silhouettes backlit by the remains of the fire.

The young one making excuses whined again. "She was tied up real good. I checked."

Another slap. The older woman wielding the open palm struck with ferocious intensity. "Don't you tell me about those ties. I tightened them myself."

"Yes, Eileen."

From the tenor of Eileen's voice, she had to be in her sixties or older, yet she commanded the younger woman with the power of someone half her age. Wiry and strong, she must have been in charge. Walter sidestepped in a crouch, working his way around the periphery of the camp to get a better view.

The older woman's hair picked up the light of the dying fire and almost glowed. Stark white and long, it hung in a braid down her back. She sported jeans and boots and a jacket that appeared to be wind and waterproof. Not an idiot.

She poked a finger at the younger woman's chest. "Now you wake up Sam and the others and report back here in five minutes. We're not waiting until the morning."

The younger woman shrank back at Eileen's instructions. "What about Hampton? You said we would wait."

"Damn it, Stephanie. How stupid are you? If that

girl is gone, she's gonna tell those women all about us. Do you think they'll let Hampton stay there once they find out he's with a whole crew?"

"But we need him to tell us about the cabins. If he's been inside, he can tell us where to strike."

Walter froze. They couldn't be talking about the Clifton compound, could they? He took stock of the camp again. Vagabonds, the lot of them. No way they could mount an attack against Barry, Anne, Tracy and the kids.

"Nonsense. With that girl gone, they'll be ready for us. We have to attack now, before they have a chance to prepare. Two women and a handful of kids won't be able to stop us if we go in all together."

Walter's blood ran cold. From the way the women talked, Barry wasn't around.

Stephanie dropped her voice. "What if something goes wrong?"

Eileen reached out with her hand and the young woman flinched. She patted where she'd struck the woman only minutes before. "You know I'll always take care of you. We will get those cabins. We'll have a place to sleep and all their food and then Eileen will make you feel good. Don't you worry about that."

"Yes, Eileen." The younger woman scurried off and Walter clenched his jaw.

These women and their crew threatened Walter's family. They had kidnapped Brianna or Madison. They wanted to take what he had and what the Cliftons worked so hard to build. While Walter had been off hunting and gathering and taking his time, his family needed him.

He cursed himself for leaving.

Why had he thought they were safe here? Why had he assumed the worst was over? He saw it in the cities. He heard it from Colt and Larkin. People were desperate. The ones who already knew how to hustle and survive and bend the law were better suited to survive in a land where taking kept you eating, drinking, and gave you shelter.

Hell, hadn't he done the same thing? Hadn't they all done the same thing? The country would devolve into haves and have-nots and the nots would always be hustling to change their status. People like Eileen and her little gang would always be coming and trying to steal what they couldn't produce.

Nowhere would ever be far enough away. Nowhere would ever be safe.

As he watched Eileen stir the embers, Walter unslung his rifle from his shoulder. He would end this right here, right now. Easing down onto one knee, he bent his head to the sights. His breath sawed from his lungs.

A child entered his sight. *Shit*. Walter pulled his finger off the trigger as a little thing no older than three bounded up to the old woman. Eileen scooped her up into her arms and stood up.

"Hey, there, sweetie pie. What are you doing up in the night?"

"Mama says we go. Boom, boom. Get a house."

Eileen laughed. "Yes, baby. In a few hours, we'll

have all we could ever ask for." She set the child back down and patted her on the bottom. "Now go back to the tent or Auntie Eileen will have to give you a spanking."

Hell. Walter knew he should shoot the woman now. He had a chance. But with a little kid running around? He wasn't that much of a monster. The rise of chatter and people began to fill the camp as Stephanie did what Eileen instructed.

Men and women clambered out of tents and out from under sheets and approached the now-extinguished fire. Walter counted ten, including three children.

He needed to diffuse the threat and stop their attack before it started, but one man against seven adults wasn't good odds. Unless he killed them all, right this minute, he couldn't stop them alone.

Walter cursed himself again. Either he ran straight to the cabins and helped his family prepare, or he ran back for Colt, Dani, and Larkin.

Dani still needed help. If she didn't get to the cabins soon, she might die. He thought about all the blood that covered her body when he shined the light across her unconscious form. Her death would hang like a yoke from his shoulders.

Colt deserved his help, but Walter's family and the Cliftons did, too. It was an impossible choice. Walter scrubbed his face.

Between his family and the Cliftons, they had a gun for everyone and a decent supply of ammo. But Colt and Larkin had an arsenal. Tracy, Madison, and

Brianna were good with a gun, but Colt and Larkin were experts.

A little boy of ten or so ran through the camp, a towel tied around his neck like a superhero. Walter slunk back further into the forest. If he wanted to give those kids a chance, he couldn't massacre their parents.

He glanced up at the camp again. Seven adults so far, plus the missing man they called Hampton. With five tents, they could have as many as fifteen. Fifteen adults versus Walter, Tracy, Anne, and the kids. They could defend the compound, but people would die. Maybe some of their own.

If he enlisted the help of Colt and Larkin, he might be able to diffuse the situation before it got that far. He could keep those kids alive and their parents, too.

They couldn't kill everyone who tried to take what they had; pretty soon the entire area would be full of dead bodies.

Walter stood up and retraced his steps around the camp to the north. If he hurried, he could make it back to Colt and Larkin before Eileen and her thugs set off for the cabins. Those kids deserved a chance to grow up instead of die out here in the woods.

With a heavy exhale, Walter broke into a run.

CHAPTER TWENTY

COLT

Northern California Forest
2:00 a.m.

COLT PRESSED THE DAMP CLOTH TO DANI'S ARM AND softened the dried blood. It had been hours since Walter left on foot for the Cliftons' compound. Based on what he'd explained, the man should be back any minute, but Colt refused to take any more chances.

He wasn't going to wait it out and sit around to be rescued. Pulling the cloth away from her arm, Colt inspected the damage. Four angry gashes stood out against Dani's pale skin. The bear had mauled her forearm while she'd held it up in defense.

Thankfully, the cuts weren't to the bone, but they were deep and needed stitches. Combined with the gash on her head, she was all torn to pieces. Colt still blamed himself. He glanced up. Larkin, too.

"How's the litter coming?"

Larkin grunted as he stripped another branch from a sapling he'd hacked down in the forest. "It's coming. I'll have it together soon."

"Good."

Colt made his way to Dani's pack and tugged it open. Past the collections of dried roots and leaves Dani carried for Walter, Colt found a change of clothes. Originally Melody's, the pants and shirt would be better than the blood-soaked mess she currently wore. He made his way back over and untied her boots.

So many people were gone. So many dead. He thought of the redheaded flight attendant he left behind at the University of Oregon. Was she still alive? Was Jarvis taking care of her?

Colt snorted in disgust and tugged Dani's boots off before doing the same with her blood-soaked jeans. He stared at the sweatshirt the girl loved so much. It was beyond repair. Even if he dunked it in a raging river, he could never get the bear's blood out of it.

Pulling a knife from his own pack, Colt cut the soaked fabric away. Dani was such a fighter. That she managed to kill the bear before it mauled her to death was incredible. If only he'd been there to stop it.

He finished removing her ruined clothes and cleaned the blood from her skin as best he could. Thankfully, it wasn't hers. She suffered no further cuts or gashes apart from her arm. She was damn lucky.

"I think it's ready."

Larkin's voice startled Colt out of his thoughts and

he dressed Dani as carefully and efficiently as he could. She would need a soak in some water and disinfectant, but this was a start.

He plucked the strips of tape he'd pre-cut off the edge of his pack and used them like Band-Aids on her head and arm. After a few minutes, he sat back on his heels. "All right. I've cleaned up the most of it. Assuming she's not lost too much blood from her head, she might pull through."

All she needed to do was wake up.

Colt slipped his arms under Dani's body and lifted her limp form off the ground. He carried her over to the litter and set her down on top. Larkin had fashioned it out of layers of ponchos, two saplings, and a bunch of rope. It wasn't the most attractive, but it would do the job.

"Let's get this show on the road."

"You're sure you don't want to wait for Walter?"

Colt nodded.

"Something's gone wrong, hasn't it?" Larkin slipped his arms beneath the straps of his pack and hauled it onto his back before bending down and turning Walter's pack around. He eased Walter's pack onto his front and stood up on shaky legs.

Colt mimicked him, doing the same with his pack and Dani's. Between them, they carried hundreds of pounds and had to add Dani to the mix. It wouldn't be an easy trek.

He grunted as he reached for the litter. "That's my guess. I expected a Jeep's headlights an hour ago."

"Same." Larkin grabbed the rear of the litter and hoisted it into the air. He didn't curse, but Colt knew the man wanted to.

After a few steps of tugging and pulling and almost falling over, they found a rhythm. It was dark and treacherous and they wouldn't go faster than a snail uphill, but it was progress.

Colt offered an olive branch. "Sorry I got in your face over Dani. I know it wasn't your fault."

"Don't apologize. I deserved all your grief and more. I shouldn't have left her."

"She can be a stubborn bastard."

"That she can. But I shouldn't have listened to her."

"True." Colt adjusted his grip on the wood and sucked in a breath. He couldn't tell if what he was seeing in the distance was real or a mirage. "Larkin."

"I see it."

A little orb of light bounced and bounded through the woods at a fast clip. As Colt watched, it grew larger and larger. Whoever was out there was headed straight for them.

He eased the litter to the ground and Larkin did the same. Pulling his Sig from his belt, Colt waited.

"Colt! Larkin!" Walter's voice cut through the trees and Colt exhaled in relief.

"I could have put a bullet in your chest. Where's the Jeep?" Colt slipped the packs off his body as Walter rushed up to them.

Walter stopped in front of Colt, huffing and panting and out of breath. "Couldn't get to it. We've got a bigger problem." He wiped at his brow with his sleeve before continuing. "There's a camp five miles south of here. They're planning to attack the Clifton place."

"When?"

"Now."

Shit. Colt ran a hand through his hair and glanced down at Dani. They couldn't take her into a firefight like this. "How many? What's their skill set?"

"Seven adults, three children. Appear to be led by an older woman. She's got to be in her sixties, maybe older."

Larkin chuffed, but Walter waved him off.

"Don't discount her. The woman's as tough as nails. She's ordering the rest around like a drill sergeant."

"Weapons?"

"Don't know."

"Will they send scouts, snipers? What are we up against?"

Walter hesitated. "They don't appear to have any training. It'll be a ragtag attack."

"Then why didn't you just take them out?"

Walter's brow knit together. "They have children. A couple as young as three, another who looked to be about ten. I couldn't just start shooting."

Colt frowned and thought back to the man and his daughter in the apartment in Eugene. He couldn't kill them, either. He couldn't leave an orphan to starve to death and he couldn't kill her father and expect her to come with him, either.

He glanced down at Dani. "What's the plan?"

"We leave Dani here and hit the trail as hard and as fast as we can. If we can get to the camp before they head out, we can disarm them. Convince them not to attack."

"And if they refuse?"

Walter's eyes flicked in Larkin's direction before returning to Colt. "Then we kill them. But I want to give them a chance to do the right thing. The kids deserve it."

Larkin scratched at his beard. "This could all go to shit and you know it. Just because they have kids, doesn't mean they won't shoot first."

"I'm aware of the risks. That's why I want us to intercept them."

A million different outcomes flashed through Colt's mind. Orphaned kids. Injuries. Fires. A total loss. What if the interlopers were more competent than Walter believed? What if they destroyed the Clifton compound?

"I wouldn't have hightailed it back here if I didn't need your help. This is the best option."

Colt focused on Dani. "If we leave her here, she could die."

"If there's no cabin to come back to, is that any better?"

Damn it. Colt ground his teeth together. "Fine. But we go in light and we go in hot."

"I'm not killing any kids." Larkin unzipped the pack at his feet and pulled out the beginnings of an arsenal. "That's where I draw the line."

"Hopefully we won't have to kill anyone."

Colt snorted at Walter. "I applaud your optimism."

Walter narrowed his eyes. "If you don't want to participate, I can head back alone."

"No. We'll come and we'll help, but you need to understand the conditions. They open fire, I won't hold back."

Larkin agreed. "I'm not getting killed to save a stranger's kid. If they're willing to attack the Cliftons' place, I'm treating them like an enemy regardless of their family makeup."

Colt nodded in appreciation. He understood the desire to protect innocent children, but it couldn't be at the risk of their lives or those of the rest of the group. Walter of all people should understand that. "It's your family we're protecting, Walter. Remember that."

"Believe me, I do. And I've done my fair share of fighting the last six weeks. But I won't go in there shooting first. Not when we might be able to send them on their way without killing."

"Fine." Colt wasn't sure he agreed. Every time he tried to do the right thing, someone died. Usually the wrong someone. He knelt beside Dani. "Let me get her comfortable. Then we can go."

While Colt moved the litter to a spot beneath a tree with a thick canopy and a bit of shelter from surprise rain, Larkin pulled rifles and shotguns and pistols from the packs. He assembled them all on the ground in piles along with extra magazines and boxes of ammo.

Walter pulled a smaller pack out of his main bag

and loaded it with some of the weapons. Larkin strapped rifles to his back and shoved magazines in every pocket until his pants bulged and the seams threatened to burst.

Colt checked Dani's pulse. Still faint, but regular. He hoped like hell she would be alive when he got back. He put a rifle and a handgun in her lap. He wished Lottie had been there, but the little dog was nowhere to be found. While they had waited for Walter, Colt and Larkin took turns looking for her, but turned up nothing. He had to admit she was probably gone.

He stood up with a heavy heart. "I'm ready."

Larkin stared Dani. He pulled the rifles off his back. "I can't do this. I'm staying."

"What?"

"I owe it to Dani. I left her last time and look what happened."

Colt frowned. Without Larkin, would they be able to dissuade the crew not to attack? He glanced at Walter and could see the man thought the same thing.

Damn it to hell. Life sucked. He shook his head. "You can't stay this time. We need you. The faster we take them down, the faster we can get back here."

"What if she dies? What if another bear attacks?"

"It's a risk we have to take."

Larkin frowned. "I still feel responsible."

"Then help us defuse the threat. We'll come back with the Jeep and get her."

Colt arranged the packs around Dani in a tight little group.

"We need to go." Walter's words were clipped with urgency. "Now."

Colt nodded. "Let's do this."

He glanced once more at Larkin before following Walter toward the Clifton compound and the danger that lay ahead. He hoped like hell Dani would still be alive when he got back.

CHAPTER TWENTY-ONE

TRACY

CLIFTON COMPOUND
   3:00 a.m.

TRACY WAS RUNNING ON FUMES. SHE HADN'T SLEPT IN goodness knew how many hours. Adrenaline and fear were the only things keeping her on her feet.

She paced the kitchen while Anne and Brianna argued over what to do. Pretty soon it wouldn't matter. Hampton's little gang in the woods would be coming.

"We need to go to them and strike first. We can't risk them wrecking anything we've worked so hard for, Mom."

Brianna's harsh words were met with a shake of Anne's head. "If we run out into the forest, we're on their turf. We should wait here and defend our property. We know it better than anyone."

A moan sounded from along the far wall and Tracy rushed to her daughter's side. "Madison, honey. You're home."

Her daughter's nose twitched. "Our house is gone, Mom." Madison's eyes peeled open one by one and she blinked the room into focus.

"Brianna rescued you. You're safe."

Madison eased her elbows back, about to sit up, when Tracy pressed a hand on her shoulder. "Don't sit up. You might faint."

Her daughter lay back down and reached a tentative hand up to her head. Where the matted clumps of blood used to be, now a bandage covered the wound. She turned her head and caught a glimpse of Brianna standing by the kitchen counter. "How did you find me?"

"Lucky guess."

"You need to rest and conserve your strength. You lost a lot of blood."

"No. We need to go." Madison shrugged off her mother's hand and sat up. "The people at the camp are coming. They want this place and they won't take no for an answer."

Tracy nodded. "We know."

"Then what are you waiting for? Get out there and stop them."

Tracy glanced at Anne. "We're trying to decide the best strategy."

"What are you talking about? The only strategy we should have is stopping them."

Anne stood up from her seat at the kitchen table and made her way over to the cot where Madison now sat. "Your mother seems to think we should go to them. I think we should defend the property."

Tracy watched her daughter. At first, she opened her mouth to protest, but after a moment, she sagged against the wall. "They aren't organized. It's a hodgepodge of tents and tarps and I don't know what else."

"According to the man who came here, they're all under the thumb of one woman."

"They are. She's old, but tough."

"Brianna said there are ten."

Madison nodded. "But a few are kids. One boy was about ten, then there's two little girls. They're barely out of diapers."

Brianna stepped forward. "They won't be bringing the kids with them to attack. What if two of us scout it out and wait for them to leave? We can capture the kids and hold them hostage."

Tracy shook her head. "They won't care."

"Of course they will!"

Tracy flashed a sad smile at Anne. "They're drug addicts. Hampton hit me up for oxy. Said their leader Eileen promised they could turn this place into a lab."

"You can't be serious."

Madison agreed. "My mom's right. I was listening to two of the women when they thought I was unconscious. The leader promised they could get high if they took this place over."

Anne wrapped her arms around herself. "They've got children."

"Doesn't stop people." Tracy glanced at her daughter. She'd never shared her past in any sort of detail with Madison, but she knew all too well the lengths mothers would go if they needed a fix. "Once you're an addict, you're always an addict. The addiction owns you forever."

"Some people beat it. They get sober."

She nodded. "And some don't. You have to want to stop. You have to want to change." She exhaled and focused on Anne. "These people don't want to do either."

Anne lapsed into silence, her eyes clouding over as she thought about what Tracy and Madison said. At last, she lifted her head. "Then the goal should be to rescue the kids."

"What? Mom, that's insane."

"Is it?" She turned to Brianna. "If these people dragged their children out into the woods and are living little better than animals, we should help them. If they won't listen, at least we could help their children."

"Dad would check you for a concussion right now."

"Your father isn't here. I am. And I can't in good conscience tear these families apart."

Tracy understood Anne's reservations, but she knew how bad it could get. She knew what a desperate, addicted woman would do to service her need. "What if they attack?"

"Then we fight back. But we need to save the kids. They're innocent."

Tracy didn't possess the same optimism, but she couldn't argue. They would try to save the kids. But if it came down to them or the people standing in the cabin, Tracy wouldn't hesitate. She would protect her daughter, Brianna, and Peyton no matter what.

Tucker's death would forever haunt her. She refused to lose another member of their little family now. Especially over some stranger's kid. Those people chose to drag their children into this mess. They were the ones planning to attack. They were the ones who wanted death on their hands, not Tracy.

She would give as good as she got and then some. Her own daughter deserved that and more. With a heavy heart she walked over to the table and picked up the rifle she'd deposited there earlier in the night. "If we're going to defend this place, we need to get ready."

Brianna nodded. "I'll raid the weapons locker. We can set up a perimeter and wait for them to arrive."

Madison struggled to get up. "I want to help."

"No, honey. You need to stay here and rest."

"Mom. I'm awake and strong enough to hold a gun."

"You blacked out a few hours ago. You have a concussion."

Madison bit her lower lip in frustration. "Then at least give me a rifle. I can watch from here and give you some backup."

Tracy exhaled. There would be no talking Madison out of helping. "Fine. But I don't want you leaving this cabin."

Madison wrinkled her nose. "Okay."

Brianna picked up her own weapon as the front door to the cabin opened. Barry Clifton froze at the threshold, his eyes wide as he took in the sight.

"Dad!" Brianna rushed him and wrapped her arms around his middle.

Anne's whole countenance changed. She walked over to her husband and gave him a sideways hug. "What are you doing here?"

He gave each woman a squeeze and they stepped back. At six foot two with a barrel chest and a full head of hair, Barry looked younger than his forty-eight years.

"Hello to you, too." He lumbered in, dragging a rolling cooler behind him, and shut the door. "I couldn't sleep out by the river. Too many owls. Why do those things have to hoot all night long?"

He smiled, but it faded as he took in all the faces around the room. "You can't all be sitting around waiting for me to come home. What's going on?"

Tracy waited for Anne. She should be the one to explain.

"There's a group of people a few miles north that set up a camp."

Barry eased his pack to the floor. "I'm listening."

"They aren't friendly."

He paused with one hand still on a strap. "What does that mean?"

Brianna spoke up. "They're coming to ambush us. They want to take the property over."

"Like hell they will." Barry stood up and pulled his pistol from a holster on his belt. "We'll drop them before they step one foot on Clifton land."

Anne stepped forward. "They have children."

"Not one of mine."

"Two of them are toddlers."

Barry raised an eyebrow. "And why is that factoring into this discussion? If they are a threat, we need to take them out. No one is coming on this property uninvited. You and I have discussed this. I thought we were in agreement."

"Mom wants to save the kids."

Barry held up a hand toward Brianna. "Give us a minute, Bri. Okay?"

Brianna crossed her arms and glowered. Tracy suppressed a smile. Brianna might be twenty, but she was still their daughter.

Barry lowered his voice and pulled Anne over to the corner of the room. Tracy couldn't hear the words, but from the look on Anne's face and the way she threw up her hands, it didn't seem to be going her way.

Tracy busied herself checking Madison's head injury and trying not to fidget. Brianna walked over and sat on the other side. She couldn't take her eyes off her parents and Tracy couldn't blame her.

Every minute that ticked by lowered their ability to prepare. Peyton was the only current guard on duty. He wouldn't be able to hold back a mob. They needed to get on with it.

At last, Barry and Anne pulled away from the wall. The big man stalked over to Tracy, Madison, and Brianna. "I think Bri's idea has merit. Two of us can hit the camp from the other side and take whoever stays behind hostage."

Tracy shook her head. "It won't work. These people don't care about their kids."

"I'm not intending to barter with them."

"Then what's the point?"

Barry's lips thinned into a line. "No one is coming to take this place. I plan to shoot to kill."

"I don't follow."

"We need to keep the kids away from what's going to happen here. If they become orphans, they'll need a place to stay."

Tracy blinked as she processed the full import of Barry's words. "You mean you don't want them to watch their parents die."

"Exactly."

Tracy swallowed. When Barry laid it all out in the open, it sounded horrific. But it was exactly what she'd been advocating. The adults couldn't be trusted. But the kids…

They had a chance to change.

She hated what she was about to say, but it was the truth. "I'll go. I can keep the kids safe and if there are any adults left behind…"

"We can take care of it." Brianna stepped forward. "Together we can make sure the kids are safe and out of harm's way."

"It will be dangerous. You could meet them on the way in. They could catch you out there unaware."

Brianna glanced at Tracy. "We can handle it."

Barry nodded. "Good. Then the three of us and Peyton will protect the property." He glanced around. "No word from Walter?"

"Not yet."

"It would be nice to have his support."

"You're telling me." Tracy shoved the yearning for her husband aside. It wouldn't be the first fight he'd missed. She exhaled and settled her nerves. "Let's get ready. We don't have time to spare."

CHAPTER TWENTY-TWO

TRACY

NORTHERN CALIFORNIA FOREST
4:30 a.m.

TRACY AND BRIANNA SLOWED AS THEY NEARED THE SPOT where they left Hampton Rhodes a few hours before.

"What should we do with him?"

"Take him with us, I suppose. We can't leave him for the rest of the group to find."

Brianna's curls bounced as she nodded.

So far they hadn't seen a single glimpse of anyone from the camp headed their way. Their plan was to secure Hampton and then track wide around the camp to attack it from the north. If Eileen and her gang were still there, all the better.

As the area with the rock outcrops came into view, Tracy slowed. "You snake around the east, I'll come at the tree from the west."

Tracy waited until Brianna disappeared into the dark pre-dawn light and eased toward the area she left the man. It didn't take long to find the remains of the rope and wadded-up T-shirt she'd used as a gag.

Brianna joined her moments later. "What the hell?"

Tracy shrugged. "He's gone."

"Do you think they're already on the attack?"

"We have to assume the worst."

"Then let's hurry. We can't waste any more time." Brianna picked up the pace and Tracy followed. They had to get to the camp and assess the situation.

Anne would never forgive them if the children died in whatever firefight came next. Tracy had to admit a small part of her agreed. The kids wouldn't understand if they watched their parents die. It would terrify them and change their lives forever, even if getting a chance to grow up out from under the pall of drug addiction would be a better life.

But Tracy wasn't a judge or a jury. She didn't want to be the person to make that decision. She glanced at Brianna and leaned close enough to whisper. "Are you okay with bringing the kids home?"

"It's better than leaving them out here to starve to death." Brianna hoisted her rifle up a bit higher in her grip. "But I'd rather these people just take their kids and leave."

"Me, too."

The first hint of a tent came into view in the dark and the women fell silent. Tracy checked her rifle for the hundredth time. *I can do this.* Even if the kids were traumatized at the sight of the weapons, it would be better to contain them there. Anne had been right about that.

Brianna angled away to the right and Tracy crept forward, eyes wide for any movement in the dark. She half expected a flurry of activity: young people running about with guns and grenades as they banded together to take everything the Cliftons worked so hard to have.

But there was nothing. No sound. No movement. Not even a child crying.

She stepped into the camp and surveyed the scene. *Chaos.*

A tent sagged against a tree, torn open and spewing its contents all over the ground. A sheet lay in a tangled mess, trampled with footprints and smears of dirt. She bent to pick up a crushed beer can. Black burn marks and soot coated the underside and a dent in the top told Tracy all she needed to know. Drugs. Again.

Had Eileen given them all something to prepare for battle? Or did Hampton escape and make it back before they took off? Was there a celebration when he arrived a free man?

Tracy stood up and made her way through the wreckage, kicking over empty soda bottles and remains of sleeping bags. Something small and furry caught her eye and she paused. She reached down picked it up. A teddy bear. With one arm torn almost completely off and stuffing bursting from the seam, it wasn't much to look at. But it reminded her of their mission.

The children. Where were the two little ones Madison said were running around early that night? What about the boy who smiled at her daughter?

Tracy wedged enough of the bear into the back pocket of her jeans that it would stay put. If she found the child it belonged to, it would smooth over the impending catastrophe.

Brianna walked into the middle of the camp, no longer attempting to hide. "They're gone. Every last one of them."

Tracy stood up. "Any sign of the kids?"

"Not a one."

She pulled the bear out of her pocket and showed it to Brianna. "They left in a hurry. No way a little girl wouldn't bring her teddy bear."

Brianna swallowed. "You don't think…"

"I don't have any idea. Drug addicts can do terrible things."

"I take it you know from personal experience?"

Tracy nodded. "I know exactly what those kids are going through. My mother—" Tracy looked away. "Let's just say she wasn't the best role model."

"Then we need to get back and warn the others."

Tracy paused. Something about the whole thing didn't feel right. Where were they? They should have run into the gang of them in the forest. Did they get lost? Veer off track to the Cliftons' place? Did Hampton do the right thing and lead them the other way?

There were so many viable scenarios.

She looked up at the sky. The faintest blue hinted at the horizon. Sunrise was still hours away, but the forest anticipated it. Tracy did, too. They would have visibility and vantage points and the ability to defend themselves in the light.

Now they were just targets.

"You're right." She turned to Brianna. "Let's go."

As Tracy turned south, she froze. Was that an animal? She swore she heard a rustling in the leaves. She motioned for Brianna to get down.

They both sank into a crouch.

"What?"

Tracy brought her finger up to her lips and pointed in the direction of the noise.

Brianna nodded and inched toward the tree line just outside the small clearing occupied by the tents and wrecked fire. Tracy stayed still, listening.

There it was again.

A small, warbled crunching, almost as if someone were rolling their feet through cheerios. She eased closer to Brianna and the cover of the trees.

"Stay where you are!"

The sound of a strange man's voice sent Tracy into survival mode. She dropped to the ground and rolled in Brianna's direction as a shot rang out from the tree line.

Brianna was taking pot shots into the dark. She wouldn't hit the target, but it might keep the man at bay.

A tree loomed in front of Tracy and she scrambled to take cover behind it. Who was out there? Had they taken out the camp? Did one of the men stay behind?

Tracy's heart pounded. She had to keep Brianna safe. The girl was liable to step out guns blazing and start a war. She eased closer to where Brianna stood, body protected by a thick tree. "Did you get a look at him?"

"No." Brianna kept her head bent and eye lined up with the sight. "Doesn't mean I can't shoot him."

A firefight was the last thing they needed. "We don't even know who they are."

"Drop your weapons."

The steely male voice came from way too close and the opposite direction. Tracy turned around in slow-motion. A man stood no more than three paces away, pistol aimed straight at her chest. He had that look about him Tracy remembered from her days as a Marine wife.

Hard-ass military. No room for bullshit.

She lifted her chin. "Give me one reason why we should."

"How about fifteen?" He lowered his head and took aim.

Tracy held out the rifle.

"What are you doing?" Brianna hissed the question.

"Keeping us alive."

"He'll shoot us anyway."

The man's lips twitched. "I can hear you."

"So?" Brianna stood with her rifle still pointed at the man. "It's the truth. I give you my weapon and I'm a sitting duck."

"You are anyway, babe."

"I'm not anyone's babe."

"Give me the rifle."

"Not a chance."

He reached for the gun Tracy still held out in front of her. She could have extended her reach and made it easier on the man, but she refused. The closer he came, the more of a chance she had to take him out.

The man leaned in and Tracy twisted the rifle at the last minute, attempting to hit him square in the gut. He dodged and sidestepped up to her, closing the distance between them before she could recover.

The barrel of the pistol etched a cold circle on her temple as he pressed it tight to her skin. "I said give it to me, not punch me with it."

She kept her voice even. "My mistake."

He took the rifle from her hands and frisked her, removing the handgun lodged in her waistband before stepping back. "Now, you. Hand it all over."

"No."

The girl was so damn stubborn. "Brianna. It's over. You'll never get a shot off."

"Listen to your mother."

"She's not my mother."

"Whoever she is, then." The man's tone slipped into frustration and Tracy tensed.

If they could distract him enough, maybe she could reach the knife in Brianna's boot.

"Why did they leave you behind? Didn't they trust you to do the job?"

The man glanced at Tracy without moving his head. "Excuse me?"

"What did you do, break Eileen's rules?"

"Lady, I don't know who or what you're talking about."

Oh, no. If he wasn't with Eileen and her gang, then who the hell was he?

CHAPTER TWENTY-THREE

COLT

Northern California Forest

5:00 a.m.

Why are all women batshit crazy? Colt pressed the barrel of the Sig tight to the one woman's head while he watched the college-aged girl for any sudden moves. He should have shot them when he first saw them, but something about the whole scene didn't sit right.

When he saw them exchange words over a damn torn-up teddy bear it broke something inside him and any thought of taking them out fled. He could handle two women without a good sense of situational awareness. At least he thought so.

But now as he stood there, gun on one and a scowl pointed at the other, he wasn't sure. They didn't strike him like the type to go all in on a pre-dawn raid. If they weren't with the group Walter came to stop, who the hell were they?

He wished Walter would hurry it up and get to the camp. Thanks to the man's trek to the campsite and back, he couldn't keep up with Colt for long. As Walter fell back, Larkin did too. So far, Colt was the only one of their group to arrive.

Reinforcements would sure be nice. He motioned to the curly haired, crazy girl. "You shoot me with that thing and the bullet will just go straight through. I'll be on you before you can scream."

"Oh, yeah? How about we try it and find out?"

"Brianna, please. You're not helping."

The young one glared at the older one.

"Brianna, huh? What kind of a name is that?"

"How about you mind your own business?"

In some weird way, Colt was almost enjoying himself. "You always let her disobey you like that?"

"She's not my daughter."

"Then who the hell are you two? Some modern-day Thelma and Louise?"

"Who?" The one named Brianna scrunched up her face, but the one closer to Colt's age suppressed a smile.

"No. She's my daughter's friend."

"I see." At least Colt wanted to, but the more they talked, the more they distracted him from what mattered: disposing of the threat.

He nodded at the rifle still in Brianna's hands. "Last time I'm going to ask. Give me the gun."

"No."

Colt snorted. He should shoot them and be done with it. "Guess we're at a stalemate, then."

"Looks like it."

Boots crunched on leaves and twigs behind Colt and he used the handgun lifted from the first woman to point in the direction of the noise.

"Whoa, don't shoot one of the good guys." Larkin held up his hands and came to a stop in the clearing.

"You grin any wider and those lips will crack."

Larkin waved at the women. "Hi, ladies. Nice to meet you."

Colt pointed at Brianna. "Cut it out and disarm her, will you?"

"Aw, you're no fun." Larkin stepped forward and the firecracker swung the rifle in his direction. "Hey, now. No sense in shooting me. All you'll end up with is a dead friend and a massive headache."

"Give him the gun, Brianna."

"Listen." Colt pressed the Sig hard enough into her head to send her back a step. "Or I'll shoot her."

After another tense moment, the younger girl finally gave up the rifle. Larkin plucked it from her hands with a flourish.

"Search her. She's liable to have a stash all over."

"Touch me and you'll regret it."

Larkin held out one hand. "Then hand them over or I won't have a choice."

Brianna reached behind her and plucked a handgun from her waistband before bending over and pulling another pip-squeak of a gun from her boot.

"Is that everything?"

She nodded and crossed her arms over her chest like a petulant child. "Now can we go? Our family is in trouble. We need to get back to them."

Colt glanced at Larkin before taking a step back. He pointed the gun at the older woman. "Is that true?"

She nodded.

"Where are you from?"

"We're not telling you that."

"Who's threatening you?"

Brianna snorted. "What, you want to be my knight in shining armor?"

Colt ground his teeth together. For once he'd appreciate it if he could have a conversation with a woman older than the age of sixteen that didn't devolve into a critique of his manliness. This was why he was single. The apocalypse changed nothing.

He exhaled. "We could help you if you weren't so obstinate."

"We could be helping ourselves if you weren't such jerks."

The other woman spoke up. "You really aren't part of the group that was here?"

Colt shook his head. "Not a chance."

"Do you know where they went?"

He shook his head. Based on the way she stared at him with a mix of apprehension and curiosity, Colt wondered what they were really after out here all alone in the forest. He opened his mouth to ask when a voice cut him off.

"What on earth?" Walter walked into the clearing, his eyes wide in disbelief.

The older woman took a step forward, but Colt brought the Sig up to her eye level. "Don't you dare."

"Colt." Walter's tone made him turn.

"What?"

"Lower the gun."

"We found them snooping around the campsite. They won't tell us where they're from or what they're after."

"They don't have to. I already know."

Colt frowned. "What are you talking about?"

"You're pointing a gun at my wife."

Colt turned back to the woman while Larkin busted out with a laugh. "You're Walter's wife?"

She held out her hand. "Tracy Sloane."

Colt lowered the gun and hesitated. Both hands held a weapon. He handed one to Larkin before giving Tracy's hand a quick shake. "Colt Potter. My apologies."

She nodded. "Understandable, given the circumstances."

Colt stepped back while Walter and Tracy reconnected. Walter wrapped his arms around his wife and his whole countenance changed. Colt glanced at the girl. "You're not their daughter?"

"No, this is Brianna. Her parents own the property we're heading to."

Colt was thankful the sun had only graced the forest with the dimmest of light. No one needed to see his burning cheeks.

"You really made an ass of yourself, man." Larkin held out his hand to the girl. "Major James Larkin. Pleasure to meet you."

Brianna stared at it with a raised eyebrow, but didn't say a word. Larkin pretended not to care.

"Where's your family? Are they safe?" Walter spoke up and all eyes turned toward him.

"They're back at the cabin." Brianna's brow pinched. "The people here—they were planning to attack."

"We know." Walter filled Brianna and Tracy in on the events of the past few hours and how they left an injured Dani alone in the woods. "We didn't know what else to do."

To hear Walter explain it brought all the pain and indecision back for Colt. He hated that she was out there alone. Tracy reached out and touched his shoulder. He jumped.

"You really put her safety on the line for us?"

Colt nodded. "Seemed like the best course of action for everyone."

"Thank you." The sincerity in Tracy Sloane's voice came through loud and clear. She turned to Brianna. "Take them to the cabins. As fast as you can, Brianna."

"What are you going to do?"

Tracy smiled at her husband. "I'm going to find Dani. I'll keep her safe until you can get to us."

Walter's eyes widened. "Are you sure? What if these people are wandering the forest?"

"I'll take the risk. She shouldn't be alone."

Colt couldn't believe a woman he just met and threatened with a gun to the head would help him. "I don't know what to say. Thank you."

She nodded. "If you're a friend of my husband,

then you're a friend of mine. Besides, you can do more to help the Cliftons than I can. We didn't even hear you approach."

"Navy SEALs are good for something." Walter grinned. "Thank you, my dear."

Tracy listened as Colt and Walter explained where Dani was located and how best to get there. Then she set off into the forest at a steady lope. With the sun finally beginning to rise, the forest wasn't as treacherous. They could make up for lost time.

Colt turned to Brianna. "Lead the way. It's time we rescue your family."

Brianna turned without another word and took off at a brisk jog. Colt sucked in a breath and prepared for a quick journey. Legs almost half his age would be tough to keep up with, but he'd do it. And he'd stop whoever was out to do Walter's group harm.

No one else would be pulling a gun on Walter's group today if Colt could help it.

CHAPTER TWENTY-FOUR

MADISON

Clifton Compound

5:30 a.m.

"Didn't you promise to stay inside?"

Madison shot Peyton some side-eye before turning her attention back to the tree line. "The front porch counts."

"Right. And we're just out here for some early morning target practice."

Shifting her position behind the woodpile, Madison brought the binoculars back up to her eyes. They had been taking turns scanning the entrance to the Clifton family property for the past half hour with no success. Had all the talk of attacking the place been fantasy? Did Tracy and Brianna engage the camp before Eileen could mount an ambush?

"You think they're waiting for full daylight?"

"Beats me. Maybe they're all tweaking too hard to find the place."

Madison frowned. After watching Eileen in action, she couldn't believe they had a change of heart. Either something held them up or their plan involved plenty of sunshine.

She thought through the options. Seven adults, eight including the man her mother left in the woods. While she had been their captive, Madison spotted a rifle and a handgun, but not much more. What could they do with a couple of guns and eight people?

"You think this is just the beginning?"

Peyton's question caught her off guard and she lowered the binoculars. "Of the attack?"

"No. Of the future. Will more people leave the cities and try to find their way out here?" Peyton shifted in his chair. "If so, we'll have to construct a perimeter. A fence or some sort of barricade. Post sentries. It'll be a challenge."

Madison brought the binoculars back up and stared at the Clifton land without really seeing anything. Before the grid failed, people were already pitted against each other. Fights on social media. Arguments over the haves and have-nots. Basic, fundamental differences of opinion on everything from politics to religion to free speech.

Was this merely an extension of the underlying strife? Madison didn't think so. This new world stripped the conflict down to the barest essentials. Food, water, shelter.

It was easier to steal than to create. It was easier to loot than to build.

She glanced at Peyton. "I wish I could disagree, but you might be right."

Peyton nodded. "All the big cities have to be chaos by now. I can't imagine what it's like in Beverly Hills."

Madison's heart ached for Peyton. The only family he ever knew disowned him right before the EMP. "Do you ever think about your dad?"

"Yeah." Peyton stared out at the trees. "He's probably dead. How long can a record exec make it without anyone to fetch his coffee, right?"

"There have to be some little towns where people are okay. Places where everyone knows everyone and they can band together to make a community." Madison straightened as the thought gave her hope. "Maybe there's even pockets in the big cities, too. Remember the community garden in Davis? I bet people are expanding it and using the catchment system for water."

"I hope you're right." Peyton lapsed into silence and Madison followed.

In the dark moments, she could fall into the trap of believing America was doomed, but she refused to stay there for long. Hope would keep them going. Hope would bring communities together.

She sucked in a breath and her nose twitched. "Do you smell that?"

Peyton rose up, his nose sticking in the air. "Is that smoke?"

Madison's eyes widened in alarm. "You don't think they would burn the place down, do you?" She brought the binoculars back up and scanned the trees. From their vantage point, they couldn't see the orchard or the fields. Those all sat behind them to the north. Barry and Anne were in charge of that side of the property.

"Should we check it out?"

"Barry told us to stay here." Madison kept the binoculars up as she searched for any movement. "We're the last line of defense for the buildings."

"I'm doing a search." Peyton eased out of his chair and readied a rifle. "If I see anything, I'll whistle."

Madison nodded. "Be careful."

She watched as Peyton eased off the cabin's porch and slinked around the side. He disappeared from view and Madison pressed her lips together. They would survive this attack. The Cliftons would not lose their home.

Madison ticked off the seconds in her head. One minute, then two, then three. No whistle from Peyton. She inhaled. Was the smell stronger? She sniffed again, but couldn't be sure.

Adjusting the zoom on the binoculars, Madison focused her attention on the bits of forest coming into view with the rising of the sun. Most of the hidden nooks beneath the trees still languished in the shadows, but here and there the darkness gave way to gray.

She squinted and leaned forward. Was that a flutter? A glint of metal in the light?

All of a sudden, her breath caught. *There! A person.* She was sure of it. Pink jacket. Blonde hair. One of the younger women; it had to be.

Madison shoved her thumb and forefinger in her mouth and blew. A piercing whistle cut the stillness.

A bird twittered and took to the sky and Madison waited. No responding whistle. No Peyton.

Where was he? She whistled again, using all her breath, hoping, praying for a response.

Nothing.

She twisted the focus on the binoculars and searched the forest. The woman at the tree line was gone.

Madison didn't know what to do. She had promised her mother to stay put, but Peyton was in trouble. The smell of smoke only grew stronger by the minute. If she stayed there, safe on the cabin's front porch, she was as good as useless.

I'm sorry, Mom. Madison eased off her chair and crept over to the edge of the wood pile in a crouch. The side of the cabin provided no cover. Twenty feet separated Madison from the wash house. Twenty feet of open grass with nothing for protection except her speed and wits. She would have to make a run for it.

With a deep breath, she launched off the porch, running as fast as her legs could carry her. Every step seemed to stretch on for a mile, every second an hour. It was as if she'd fallen into the rabbit hole and ended up in the hallway that went on forever.

A booming crack burst from the north and a bullet threw dirt and grass onto Madison's shoe. She jerked her head up in alarm and pushed harder. Diving for the cover of the wash house, Madison tore the door open as another bullet lodged in the wood siding. She ducked inside and the door slammed shut behind her.

Eileen's camp was out there and they were hunting. *Maybe that's why they waited. They wanted to pick us off one by one in the daylight.*

Madison's heart struggled to keep time with her runaway thoughts. Where were Peyton, Anne, and Barry? Had they been captured? Ambushed?

Wouldn't I have heard something?

Madison checked her rifle. Full magazine. Enough rounds to take out all the hostiles if it came to that. For a moment, she wished her father were there. Fighting side by side gave Madison courage and hope.

But it didn't matter. She would do this on her own.

"She's in there!" A muffled shout reached Madison inside the wash house. She crouched beneath the frosted window, unable to see enough to defend herself. *Why did I run in here?* It was the worst possible location to hide.

"Burn her out!"

Madison rose up in a panic. They wouldn't set fire to the cabins. Not if they wanted to take them over. She spun around in a circle. The only way out or in was the front door or the window on the side.

A shot echoed from the rear of the property and Madison leapt into action. No time to think or prepare. She had to get out of there and help her family. With a well-placed kick to the door, Madison launched it wide open before turning to the window.

The door swung on its hinges and slammed into the outside wall of the cabin before swinging all the way back around and banging into the casing. While it rocked back and forth, Madison shoved open the window.

Please let me escape without a bullet wound. Please.

Hoisting herself up, Madison eased out the window and fell to the ground. Her knees buckled and she hit hard. Air rocketed from her lungs and she struggled to breathe.

More shouts. More gunfire.

She covered her head and crouched against the side of the building, but the shots didn't pierce her skin or end her life. She peeled her arm away. No one was there. Madison took the chance and ran.

The forest loomed ahead of her, but motion caught her eye to the left. She turned to see Barry crouched down at the corner of the bunk house, rifle on his shoulder as he took aim. He fired into the tree line as more shouts erupted.

Where was Peyton? Madison ran for the trees, rifle up and ready in her hands. *I can do this. I can make it.* Her lungs burned and her head throbbed. It took all her strength to propel herself forward, but Madison refused to stop. She refused to back down.

"There she is! Get her!"

She swung in an arc, rifle up as a woman from the forest camp came into view. Madison didn't hesitate. She pulled the trigger, but the woman didn't stop. She kept right on running at her with nothing but a knife in her hand and her mouth wide open in a scream.

Madison took aim and fired again. The bullet slammed into the woman's chest dead center. She kept coming.

Was she wearing a vest? Madison fired again and again pulling the trigger four times in a row. Each bullet hit the woman in her torso, but still she didn't drop.

The gap closed between them. Thirty feet. Twenty. Ten.

Madison screamed in rage and fear and shot again. The bullet pierced the woman's skull right between the eyes. Madison didn't even wait to watch her hit the ground. She turned toward the forest and ran.

CHAPTER TWENTY-FIVE
COLT

Clifton Compound
5:30 a.m.

Brianna held up a hand and Colt slowed. "The field Madison and Peyton tilled is straight ahead about a hundred yards."

"What's beyond that?"

"A small orchard, maybe twenty trees. Then our pasture. It's only about an acre, but we're raising pigs and chickens."

"Buildings?"

"We've got a barn and a storage shed to the right of the pasture, but the living area is divided into three cabins: kitchen, bunk house, and wash house."

Colt nodded. The layout fit a build-as-you-go homestead. Start small and work up little by little until the entire place is built out. It made protecting it damn difficult. He scrubbed a hand down his face and checked his Sig. Full magazine and two more shoved in his pockets. It would be essential for any close-in fighting.

He opted to forego the rifle this time, leaving the long-distance shots to Larkin and Walter. Colt would be the front line, side by side with Brianna. Splitting up gave Colt and Larkin a chance to contribute without having to guess who was on what side. With Walter and Brianna leading the way, there would be no cases of mistaken identity.

"My dad will shoot first and never ask questions. You'll need to call out if we get separated."

"What does he look like?"

Brianna flashed a smile. "Big guy, bad attitude. Can't miss him."

Colt nodded in appreciation. A man like that would earn his respect in a heartbeat. "All right. I'm ready."

As Brianna took a step toward the property, a shot rang out. Colt grabbed her by the arm and dragged her to the ground. He'd hoped to beat Eileen's crew and set up a defense, but they weren't so lucky. "We'll have to flush out the attackers."

Brianna nodded and eased forward. Together, they crept toward the new field. As the trees thinned, a large patch of dirt opened up in front of them. Beyond it, an organized row of trees. *The orchard.*

Colt inhaled. *What is that?* He reached for Brianna. "Do your parents use wood for heat?"

She nodded. "But not during the day. And that doesn't smell like our wood."

Colt motioned toward the pasture. "Let's hurry. If there's a fire, we need to contain it."

Brianna hustled in a half-crouch, half-run around the plowed patch of dirt with Colt on her heels. A pig squealed. Chickens clucked and fluttered. The whole pasture was in commotion and panic.

Colt spotted the flames first. "There!"

Brianna's mouth fell open. "They've set fire to the chicken coop! It'll take the whole pasture with it!" She rose up to run, but Colt grabbed her arm.

"Don't. You'll get yourself killed."

She tugged against his grip. "I have to do something."

"We will. But rushing in there without a plan won't help. Where's the biggest source of water?"

Brianna chewed on her lip. "The well. It's deep water, but we don't have an easy way to pump mass quantities."

Colt frowned. "What about dirt? Do you have a wheelbarrow?"

"We have two. They're over by the shed."

"Lead the way. We can use the dirt in the open field to smother the flames. But we'll have to be quick."

Brianna took off, skirting the pasture and the orchard. She stopped at the edge. Two wheelbarrows leaned against the wall of a metal shed fifty feet away.

Colt sucked in a breath and readied himself. "Give me cover. I'll get them."

"You can't get both."

"Watch me."

Colt took off as fast as possible and reached the

wheelbarrows without incident. They were large farm versions with thick, white-walled tires and metal handles. He flipped both over in a nestled stack and threw a pair of shovels on top. Bracing himself, Colt lifted the bottom handles. The full weight came to bear on his arms and he grunted.

Nothing like a little workout under fire. He took off, running as best he could with a hundred pounds of awkward metal in his hands. A bullet hit the ground beside his feet and Colt jerked his head up.

A man crouched beside the edge of a cabin thirty yards away. Big. Mean. Calm.

Barry Clifton.

Colt shouted. "I'm with Brianna!" He scanned the forest for the girl, hoping she could see and lend a hand.

Her father took aim.

Colt swallowed. He thought about what only a friend would know. "Go Aggies!"

Barry paused and Brianna's voice hollered out. "Dad! Don't shoot!"

Brianna came flying out of the woods, blonde hair like a curly halo around her head. She stuttered to a stop in front of her dad. "The chicken coop is on fire!"

Barry stood up in a rush. "We have to stop it or the whole pasture will catch. The orchard, too."

Shouts erupted from the forest. Gunshots rang out. A bullet hit the side of the wheelbarrow. Colt flipped them on their side and crouched behind them. Barry and his daughter ducked behind the side of the building.

With his head down and finger on the trigger, Barry

scanned the forest. He shouted at Colt. "Who the hell are you?"

"Walter's friend."

"Walter's back?"

Brianna peered around the corner of the building. More gunfire. "Yes. He's brought two men with him. Colt and Larkin."

"Good. We need the help."

Colt kept himself hidden by the wheelbarrow as he turned around. "I'm getting dirt from the tilled field to smother the fire."

Barry grunted his approval. "Go. I'll cover you."

Brianna rushed up to Colt's side. "I'm coming, too. You'll never be able to push two wheelbarrows full of dirt."

More shouts echoed from the woods.

"Hurry! We have to save the animals!"

Colt reached for the handles of the first wheelbarrow as Brianna did the same with the second. "Get as much dirt as you can, as fast as you can."

Brianna nodded and they took off under the cover of a volley of shots from her father.

The wheelbarrows canted and tipped and Colt almost lost the shovel, but they made it to the clearing without a bullet to the head. He grabbed the shovel and stabbed the ground, loading up the wheelbarrow as fast as possible. Brianna did the same, but at a third of his size and not nearly the same strength, she couldn't keep up.

Colt motioned to the heaping wheelbarrow in front of him. "Take mine. I'll fill yours."

"What do I do with it?" Brianna shoved her shovel into the overflowing dirt and reached for the handles.

"Use it as a break. Get the dirt on the flames that spread off the coop, nice and thick. Smother everything that spreads to the pasture. I'll be right behind you."

Brianna took off, racing as fast as her smaller legs could manage with such a heavy load. Colt hoped like hell her father could give her cover.

Scanning the tree line with every scoop of the shovel, Colt blinked the sweat from his eyes. A blur of blue caught his attention and he dropped to the ground.

A man slinked through the trees, head bouncing like a bobblehead on a dashboard. Could he be Peyton, the young man Walter told him about? Colt didn't know and he didn't want to shoot a good guy. He waited, hiding behind the wheelbarrow as the man approached.

From his choppy steps, to the way he kept scratching at his head, Colt guessed he'd spent a good many days getting high in the woods. All he needed was confirmation.

Thirty seconds later, he got it. A woman with white hair tied back in a braid emerged from the trees. She took the man by the shoulder and pointed toward the flames. *Eileen, the leader.* Colt couldn't hear the words, but he could tell by her pointing and smiles that she was pleased.

She wouldn't be once Colt took her and her minion out. With a regulated exhale, Colt took aim. He squeezed the trigger and the man crumpled to the ground. One down, six adults to go. He turned to Eileen and took aim. She dropped to the ground, using the man's body as a shield. Colt pumped five quick shots into the area before abandoning the cover of the wheelbarrow.

He ran toward the man, gun out and ready.

The body loomed ahead. *No Eileen.* Colt slowed and approached with caution, scanning the forest for any sign of the woman. Nothing.

Colt checked the man's neck. No pulse. He swiveled in a three sixty, but came up empty. Could she have escaped without a single wound? Did he miss every time?

Thanks to his training as an air marshal, Colt found that incredibly unlikely, but the evidence stared him in the face. Eileen was gone.

He turned and ran back to the wheelbarrow before shoving his gun in his waistband. Brianna needed his help. Leaving the fire to her so he could hunt down a fugitive wasn't in the cards. With a grunt, Colt grabbed the handles, hoisted up the load, and ran.

By the time he reached the fire, Brianna was dripping in sweat and soot and her wheelbarrow was empty. The flames still licked the walls of the chicken coop, turning the painted plywood and wire into a charred mess of scrap metal.

A gaggle of pigs and chickens snorted and squealed and carried on behind Brianna, but she'd managed to keep the flames from spreading. Colt set the wheelbarrow down and she attacked it with her shovel, dumping more dirt in front of the flames.

"Where is everyone else?"

"I don't know."

"What about your dad?"

"He's gone off to hunt them down."

"Your mom?"

"Haven't seen her. I think the people from the forest are as scared of the fire as the pigs."

Colt nodded. "I'll give you cover."

"No. Go find them and kill them. Every last one."

Colt regarded Brianna for a moment, then nodded. "I'll do my best."

CHAPTER TWENTY-SIX

WALTER

CLIFTON COMPOUND
6:00 a.m.

DAYLIGHT BRIGHTENED THE FOREST, FORCING WALTER and Larkin to take cover behind an outcropping of rock. While a series of gunshots rang out on the Clifton family property, Walter went on the offensive, tracking down the source of the bullets.

Between him and Larkin, they'd chased a pair of Eileen's people into a natural pen of boulders and impossible brambles. Neither could get out unless they ran by Walter, and he wasn't about to let them leave alive.

He motioned to Larkin who guarded the other side of the corral. The sooner they killed these people, the faster it would all be over. Tracy wouldn't approve of what he was about to do, but she wasn't there and this was war.

Walter eased around the rocks on his side of the entrance and Larkin did the same. The woman crouched against the rock, squeezing into an impossibly tight space, while the man paced back and forth, wagging his finger at nothing in particular and shouting at the air.

Did they really think they could go toe-to-toe with Walter, Barry, and the rest of them and come out the victors? Walter almost felt sorry for them, but then he remembered the hell they put his daughter through.

He lifted the rifle and stepped into the clearing.

The woman shrank back, snarling as she stared at him.

The man stopped walking and pointed at Walter. His fingernails were torn and bloody; his face sallow and hollow. "You! You did this! We must cast you out! You're the curse. You're the devil!"

Walter pulled the trigger. A bullet pierced the man's head and his body hung in the air for a moment, dead but still standing. As he hit the ground, the woman lunged. A knife caught the light and Walter fired.

She took the bullet like a kick to the chest and staggered back, staring down in disbelief at the blood spreading across her dirty shirt. As life fled her body, she fell, joining her friend in the leaves at Walter's feet.

He turned to Larkin. "Get to the cabins. See if they need help."

"What are you doing?"

"I'm searching for any stragglers."

Walter took off without another look behind him at the man and woman they just killed. With Larkin, Colt, and the rest of them fighting it out at the homestead, Walter kept parallel to the property line, searching the surrounding forest for any member of Eileen's party that escaped.

They would never be coming back to hurt his family.

With quiet steps, he eased through pockets of ferns and over fallen logs, around groves of tightly packed saplings and vines covered in unripe blackberries. A hawk screeched and took off into the open less than a hundred yards ahead. Walter sank into a crouch. A thicket of gangly bushes gave him cover as he crept forward. Whoever was out there would not get away.

Ahead, a hill rose in a gentle slope and Walter took his time, watching and waiting. After a few minutes of silence, he was rewarded. A flutter of leaves and another twitter of a small wren or cardinal. The hint of a shape moving in the shadows.

With the sunrise officially upon them, Water could see far enough to pick out a person up the entire slope. He wouldn't even need to move to make the kill.

He brought up the rifle and used the scope to root out the noisemaker. A flash of white caught his eye and Walter froze. *Eileen.*

She limped in agonizing slowness up the hill, twisting around every few steps to check for any pursuit. From the way she cradled her left arm it was either broken or severely injured. *Good.*

The woman deserved to suffer after what she put her group and his own through. According to Tracy,

Madison could have died. Walter wasn't letting the woman responsible slink away and nurse her wounds.

He would be the end of her. She would forever regret trying to steal what wasn't hers.

Walter slung the rifle over his shoulder and unholstered a Glock. Not his handgun of choice, but beggars and all that. He would never turn down a weapon again.

With the gun out straight and ready to fire, he closed the gap, gaining on Eileen with every step. She stumbled and Walter seized the chance, running forward without care for noise or the element of surprise.

She flailed and scrabbled against the ground, flipping over just as the barrel of his gun lined up with her face.

Walter could have pulled the trigger right then and ended it, but he paused. He owed it to his wife to try.

"Where are the kids, Eileen?"

Her face pinched and the color on her cheeks deepened. "What's it to you?"

"Let's just say I'm interested in child welfare. Unlike you."

Eileen shifted and winced as her arm flopped to the ground. Blood stained the sleeve of her jacket and the familiar hole of a bullet wound came into view. At least she'd suffered for a while.

Walter motioned to her arm. "Hurt much?"

"Like you care."

"I could fix it up. Give you something for the pain."

She stared at him, wary. "What for?"

"Tell me where those little girls are. They don't deserve to die out here."

Eileen barked out a laugh. Thanks to the leaves and dirt her white hair took on a dingy hue, but she still carried an air of toughness. "Not a chance. Those kids will get what's coming to them."

"You can't mean that. They are children."

"Their parents are traitors. You think even if you find them, that they'll let you help? Steph'll stab you in the back the first chance she gets."

Walter exhaled. If pain relief didn't convince her to talk, maybe more pain would. He pointed the gun at her foot. "How about I take away your ability to walk?"

She scrambled back an arm's length and Walter aimed at the dirt six inches to her right. He fired and her whole body jerked.

"I'm not joking here."

"Then just kill me and be done with it."

Walter stepped closer. "I don't think you understand. I'm not going to kill you, Eileen. I'm going to make you suffer. Tell me where the kids are, and I might change my mind."

Eileen spit on the ground. "Not a snowball's chance in hell. Torture me all you want, military man. I'm not tellin' you nuthin'."

Great. Just what he needed. Walter exhaled and took aim. He put a bullet right through the top of Eileen's hiking boot.

She screamed and rolled over on the ground, clutching her foot. "You bastard!"

"Tell me where they are and I'll stop."

"No."

He stepped forward again, close enough to touch her. Eileen writhed on the ground, grabbing at her foot and moaning.

Walter leaned over and pressed the barrel of the gun into the wound on her arm. He pinned her to the forest floor and dug the barrel into the entry wound of someone else's bullet.

Eileen gasped and fell back, flopping on the dirt as she struggled to breathe through the pain.

"Last chance. Tell me where they are."

She sucked in a tortured breath and nodded. "All right. Okay. I'll tell you."

With every word, her voice faded until the last barely rose above a whisper. Walter leaned in.

Eileen lunged with a shout, knife in her hand. Walter responded on autopilot. The bullet that lodged between her eyes stopped her cold.

Damn it. Walter bent to check Eileen's pulse as the knife rolled out of her hand. It was pointless. She was dead instantly.

He stood up and turned around in a slow circle. Forest stretched on for miles in every direction. Those kids could be anywhere. If all of the adults were dead...

Walter hated to think what would happen to the little girls and a boy barely old enough to take care of himself, let alone two toddlers. He kicked Eileen's limp body in frustration. She didn't deserve to die so quickly.

"Looks like you got one." Larkin's voice carried from down the hill and Walter spun around.

"The leader. She's dead."

"Good. We've got six on the property or near it."

Adding the three kids, that left two. "Where are the other two adults?"

"Don't know. No sign of the kids, either."

"Maybe they changed their minds and left."

"That's what Anne hopes."

Walter nodded. "And you?"

"I'd be fine with two fewer grown-ups causing trouble."

"Same here." Walter bent over Eileen and searched her body, pocketing the knife, but nothing else. She didn't even have a gun. He shook his head. "I tried to get her to tell me about the kids, but she refused."

"As soon as they contain the fire, Brianna's getting the Jeep ready to go get Dani."

Walter stood up. *Dani.* In the tumult of the last few hours, he'd forgotten about her tenuous claim to life and his wife's role by her side. Walter wanted them back in his sights as soon as possible. "I'll go with her."

Larkin hesitated. "Don't think there's room, I'm afraid. Colt is insisting on going."

Walter couldn't argue about that. Dani was Colt's family, not Walter's. "All right. Then let's get back home."

Larkin fell into step beside him. "It could have been worse."

"We'll see if Dani lives. Then we can talk about the what-ifs."

"Do you want to send a search party for the kids?"

Walter thought it over. "Let's wait until Tracy gets back. She should be a part of that decision."

Larkin nodded and the pair lapsed into silence. Walter hoped this was the end of the chaos for a while, but he wasn't sure that would ever happen again. Peace might become a relic of the past instead of a promise of the future.

CHAPTER TWENTY-SEVEN

TRACY

Northern California Forest

6:30 a.m.

Tracy checked Dani once again for any signs of infection. While the girl hadn't woken up, she didn't seem feverish or succumbing to any kind of sickness. With enough rest, she would likely recover. The duct tape on her head wasn't the most attractive, but Tracy had seen worse.

Walter had patched up his co-pilot the same way and even though he almost died due to an infection, antibiotics cured him. Didn't make him invincible, though.

The sun cleared the horizon and Tracy watched the forest brighten. They were sitting in a little valley between two hills, with four backpacks loaded up around them in a little circle. The sight would have been ridiculous six weeks ago, but now it made total sense.

Running her fingers over the closest bag, she thought of her husband and daughter back at the Clifton property. Had they defeated Eileen and her gang? Did they find the children? Tracy leaned back against a tree and exhaled. She could barely keep her eyes open. It had been way too many hours since she'd slept, and if Walter didn't come back with the Jeep soon, she might pass out.

Dani and all the weapons and supplies would be undefended.

At the thought, Tracy jumped up and shook out her arms and legs. *I have to stay awake.*

She stretched her arms over her head and froze. *Am I hallucinating?* She swore she heard a child cry, but as she spun around in a circle, she didn't see anything.

Tracy pulled the gun from her belt and eased away from Dani. The faint cry filtered through her ears again.

"Hello? Is anyone out there?" She stepped around a backpack and called out again. "Do you need help? Hello?"

All of a sudden, a small girl came running toward her. Blonde hair flowing in the wind, little pink dress ripped and torn. Tracy shoved her gun in the back of her waistband and crouched low. The little girl froze, eyes big and blue. Her pale cheeks offset the pink of her lips as she wiped a blob of snot from her nose. "Who you?"

Tracy smiled. "I'm Tracy. Who are you?"

"Becca! Becca come here!" A woman ran from over

the crest of the closest hill, hands outstretched for the child. The second she saw Tracy, she stumbled and cried out. "Don't hurt my baby!"

Tracy inched her way up to stand. "Are you all right?"

The woman motioned for the child again, but the little one shook her head and laughed like it was all one big game. "Na, mama. I no come. I talk Twacy."

"Hey! Steph, where the hell are you?" A man's voice called out from the same direction the woman had come.

Tracy reached behind her for the gun. She eased it from her waist, but kept it hidden behind her back.

The woman called out. "Over here, Sam."

As Sam trotted down the hill, another little girl ran ahead of him. Half-stumbling, half-skipping, she stopped beside the woman. A boy of about ten chased after her, but he retreated when he caught sight of Tracy.

All together, they were a family of five. Even with dirt and snot smearing their faces, Tracy could see the resemblance between them.

As the man approached, Tracy eyed him with wary eyes. Her gaze flitted between the children, the woman he'd called Steph, and Sam.

She spoke first. "Are you all okay?"

Steph glanced at Sam before answering. "Yeah, we're fine."

Tracy didn't want to hurt them, not in front of their children. "Are you with Eileen?"

One of the girls laughed. "Auntie Eileen is the best!"

The woman rushed in. "We're not with her anymore. We couldn't... Once we found out what she had planned, we couldn't go through with it."

Tracy glanced up at Sam. "Is that true?"

He nodded. "Are you with the group who lives here?"

"Yes."

He pointed at Dani's prone form. "Is she... Did Eileen do that?"

"She'll be fine. And no, your group isn't responsible."

"Good." Sam exhaled in relief. "Eileen told us it would be easy to make it out here. That there was a lake and a river and we could find an empty cabin and claim it as our own. We never thought she'd try to take over someone's place while they still lived in it." Sam shook his head. "We've got kids."

"Why come at all? Is where you left that bad?"

Steph chewed on her lip. "It was getting that way. When the FEMA trucks stopped coming, a lot of us freaked out."

Tracy swallowed. They had FEMA trucks?

"I worked reception at the place Eileen lived. She'd always been so nice to us." Steph reached for Sam and took his hand. "I didn't know she was into drugs."

Tracy didn't know whether to believe them or not, but they told a convincing story and they didn't take part in the fight, so that had to count for something. After a minute of awkward silence, she reached behind her with her free hand and pulled the sad little teddy bear from her pocket. One of the little girls squealed and ran up to her.

Holding it out, Tracy smiled as the little one took it and wrapped her arms around it. "Mama! She found bwear!"

Steph smiled. "Where did you find him?"

"In the camp after you were gone."

Sam tucked his brow. "She's carried that bear around with her for three years. When we couldn't find him... It was horrible."

Tracy managed a sad smile. "Are you hungry? Do you need somewhere to go?"

Sam shook his head. "We can't ask for your charity. Eileen tried to take everything from you."

Tracy bent down to the pack beside her and rummaged through it. She stood up with a bag of jerky and held it out. "Here, take it. It doesn't look like a lot, but it's calorie dense. It should tide you over for a while."

Steph took it with downcast eyes. "Thank you."

Tracy wished she could do more. She fought with herself for a moment before blurting out what she wanted to say, but knew she shouldn't. "I don't know if you'll be accepted, but I can ask the group if you can stay."

Sam shook his head. "No. We would never."

"Are you sure?"

Steph nodded. "We're going back to Truckee. It wasn't great, but it was better than out here. We're stopping by the camp, getting whatever we can, and leaving."

Tracy understood. Rural life wasn't for most people before the grid failed and she couldn't expect city dwellers to change overnight. She wished them well and watched as the two adults and three kids trundled up the next hill and out of sight.

She wondered what they would do for food and shelter while making the trek all the way back to Truckee, but it wasn't her concern. Tracy turned back around and busied herself with packing up.

Walter would be back soon with good news. She had to have faith.

* * *

7:30 A.M.

THE SOUND OF A BARKING DOG CUT THROUGH THE FOG and Tracy jerked awake. *I fell asleep.* She sat up and turned to Dani. The girl looked just as she had when Tracy sat down, unconscious and pale, but alive. The only difference was the tiny fluff ball perched beside her, yipping its little head off.

Tracy stared at the dog in confusion. Yorkshire terriers didn't roam the wilds of Northern California. She reached out a hand, but the little dog retreated closer to Dani. The entire underside of her was covered in mud and bits of leaves and her ear looked a bit mangled.

Was she Dani's dog? Tracy reached toward the nearest pack to fish out some jerky, but the scrap of a thing almost launched herself at Tracy's hand, so she backed off. "All right. I won't feed you."

The pair of them sat there staring at each other until the growl of an off-roading vehicle cut through the tension. In moments, it bounded over the rough terrain and Tracy stood, gun at the ready. *Please be Brianna.* A hint of canary yellow fender came into view and Tracy smiled.

She waited for the Jeep to slow before scrambling around the packs. It lumbered onto flat ground and Colt jumped out of the passenger side before Brianna even put the vehicle in park.

He rushed up to Dani, but froze when he saw the dog. "Lottie!" Colt bent down and scooped the pint-sized bully into his arms. "You're alive!" He turned to Tracy. "How did you find her?"

Tracy shrugged. "She found me. To be honest, I passed out a while ago. When I woke up, she was sitting beside Dani. I don't think she likes me very much."

Colt knelt beside the teenager and let Lottie onto the ground. "How is she?"

"Same as when I found her. No fever, still breathing. I think she's just worn out. We all are."

His Adam's apple bobbed as he swallowed. "You think she'll wake up?"

Tracy nodded. "She's lost a lot of blood. As soon as we get her back to the cabins, we can clean and stitch those wounds and give her some medicine. Once her body is out of crisis mode, she'll come to."

Colt stared at her, his jaw tense. "You hear that, Dani? You're going to wake up and be fine."

Tracy smiled. One minute of watching Colt tend to Dani and pet a scruffy little dog and her entire opinion of him changed. He wasn't just a gruff military man out to shoot first and never ask questions. He cared.

She looked up at Brianna. The young woman was covered in dirt and sweat, but appeared fine. "Is it over?"

"Yes. Walter found Eileen. She's dead. Hampton is, too. We counted four others killed on the property." Brianna hesitated. "Two adults and three kids are missing."

"No, they're not." Tracy pointed up the hill. "They came through here on their way back to Truckee. They never wanted to be a part of the raid. As soon as Eileen announced what they were doing, they left. It was a family."

Brianna frowned. "You let them go?"

"I wasn't killing a mother and father in front of their young children."

"We can watch for them," Colt volunteered. "If they come back, I'd expect them to be obvious."

Tracy nodded. "The little ones aren't the quietest hikers."

Brianna sighed. "Whatever. I'm too tired to deal with it now. Let's load up the gear and Dani and get back home. My dad wants a meeting."

Tracy glanced at Colt. She assumed he would be discussing whether the three newcomers could stay. Thanks to their generosity today in stopping the attack, and their willingness to leave Dani alone to accomplish it, Tracy hoped it wasn't much of a debate.

She walked over to the litter Dani still rested on and waited for Colt.

"On one."

They lifted together and carried Dani over to the Jeep before sliding her into the backseat. Lottie scrambled in after and snuggled right up next to the girl. Tracy smiled. They were going home.

CHAPTER TWENTY-EIGHT

MADISON

Clifton Compound

3:00 p.m.

Madison squeezed into the space between Peyton and her mom on the cot.

"Hey! I might be tiny, but I still have a backend!" Brianna gave Peyton a shove.

He turned to Madison, eyebrows raised, but it was her mother who spoke up.

"Just squish closer to me, dear. Unfortunately, this seat of mine's a bit bigger than it was at twenty, but we can all fit."

Madison smiled and eased in a bit tighter. "Thanks, Mom."

Her mom wrapped an arm around her shoulders and squeezed. "Have I told you how thankful I am that you're okay and back home?"

"Only a million times."

"I mean it." Her mom hugged her once more before letting go.

Madison thought about all the things that could have gone wrong over the past few days. If that camp hadn't sent a man into scout, they would have never known about Eileen and her plans. If her father hadn't come back with two military men in tow, they might not have survived.

Madison glanced over at the two men standing inside the door. From what Brianna said between hauling buckets of water to douse the chicken coop, Colt had been the one to keep the fire from spreading. Peyton said similar things about Larkin. When he'd come across the man in the woods, they worked together to secure the rest of the property without hesitation.

If her dad vouched for them, then Madison knew they would be good additions to the group, but it wasn't her choice to make. Thanks to their help, everyone in their little group survived.

She hoped some of the luck would rub off on Dani. Between the head wound and the gash on her arm she looked like an actress in a horror film. Madison reached up and felt the bandage on her own head. Maybe they all were.

Barry Clifton interrupted her thoughts with a voice loud enough to carry through the entire cabin. "Now that we're all here, we should get down to business."

He leaned forward in his chair and rested his elbows on his knees. "Thanks to everyone's hard work, we're alive and the property is secure. But I think this entire episode has changed the way we do business. We aren't an island in the woods anymore. People will be coming and when they see what we have, they will want to take it. We need to be ready for another event like this."

Madison shuddered. She knew Brianna's father was right, but she wished it wasn't true.

After speaking a bit more about the threats and how underprepared they were for something like this, he opened it up to the floor. "Anyone have ideas on what we can do?"

Peyton spoke up. "We should have constant surveillance. We could start with sentries or patrols. If we can find an electronics store that isn't smashed to bits in town, we could get some cameras and find a way to hook them into the solar panels."

Brianna chimed in. "We can't have so many people gone at once. Without you and Mr. Sloane, we didn't have enough people to defend us."

Her father nodded. "Good points, both of you. Which brings us to another issue. Colt Potter and James Larkin." He nodded at both men. "Thanks to their help today, we came out of this with only minimal damage. Walter has asked if they can join the group."

Madison glanced at her father. So far, he'd been quiet, content to lean against the wall and watch. She knew he struggled with what had happened. After being gone when the EMP hit, he had promised to never put them in the same position again.

But how could he have known about Eileen? She didn't blame him for being gone, and it all worked out in the end.

Brianna's mother spoke up. "We have room here for twelve. The more people, the more load on everything from the composting toilet to the solar panels and the well. But we built this place with the future in mind. It's not the most spacious of sleeping arrangements, but we have the room." She smiled at her husband. "And we could use the help."

Colt spoke up for the first time. "I appreciate your generosity, ma'am. But I do not want to impose. If you don't think we're a good fit or don't have the room, we understand." He glanced at Larkin before continuing. "If we do stay, we will contribute. I'm not one for sitting around and being idle." He almost grinned. "That's what's gotten me to this point, I'm afraid."

Larkin nodded. "Colt's right. Neither one of us is good at being lazy, so if we're here we want to work."

Madison's father pushed off the wall. "From what I've seen of these men, they're good people, proficient with defense, and don't put up much fuss. They're an asset, not a liability."

Mr. Clifton nodded. "Anyone else?" When no one volunteered, he slapped his thigh and leaned back. "That settles it, then. You are welcome to stay."

Colt nodded. "Thank you."

"As soon as you start patrols, we can help." Larkin glanced at Colt. "We've done our fair share of that sort of thing."

"I was hoping so." Mr. Clifton launched into a discussion on the best way to defend the property with Madison's father, Colt, and Larkin all contributing.

Hearing the four of them talk, Madison was

thankful for the new additions to the group. They had skills and knowledge Madison, Peyton, and her mom didn't possess.

"What about supplies?" Colt turned to Brianna's mom. "Are you good or do you need more?"

"We always need more. And if we're setting up a defense, cameras would be a good option. We've got the solar capacity."

"When we were on the way here we had to leave a tremendous amount behind." Madison's father nodded at Colt. "Thanks to his shoveling skills, we buried it all about twenty miles from here."

Peyton spoke up. "Brianna and I can go get it if you can show us the way."

Madison's father nodded.

"Hiking here, I got to thinking about warehouse delivery and how most big box stores have massive distribution centers." Colt ran a hand over his chin. "Most of them don't look like much from the outside."

Brianna's father leaned back. "I'm listening."

"We could organize a group and hit one. They'll have everything from toilet paper to macaroni to car batteries."

"You really think there are any left that haven't been ransacked?"

Colt shrugged. "It's worth a shot."

Brianna's father thought it over. "We've been too small to take on that kind of risk, but it's a solid idea. There's a big warehouse district on the edge of Truckee. We could start there."

"What about Cunningham's group? They're all over that side of town."

"There's got to be factions all over."

Colt spoke up. "I know the risks and Larkin and I are pretty good at urban survival." He grinned at the man. "Besides, we're a bit more expendable."

"Speak for yourself, air marshal. I tend to like breathing."

The room broke into laughter and the meeting was over. They had gained three new members, one of whom wouldn't be moving off her bed in the bunk house for a while.

As Madison braced to stand an orange ball of fluff sprang up into her lap. Fireball meowed and bumped his head against her hand. "Hey there, little man." Madison rubbed behind his ears as the cat settled in.

"Looks like he wants you to stay."

"I guess so."

As Anne opened the door to head outside a little streak of brown and gray tore into the room. It scampered across the wood floor and stopped at Madison's feet, yipping and barking and spinning in circles.

Her mom laughed. "Someone is a bit jealous." She bent down and scooped up Lottie into her arms. The Yorkie turned around on her mom's lap and plopped down, nose a few inches from Fireball.

"I thought she didn't like you?"

"Turns out she can't resist duck jerky. One bite was all it took."

Brianna leaned over. "I thought Yorkies hated cats."

Madison shrugged. "Guess she likes being here more."

Lottie and Fireball eyed each other, neither hissing nor barking. Colt walked over shaking his head. "So, a few hours here and you've found a new person, huh? Guess I shouldn't be surprised. I'm not very good with pets."

Madison's mom smiled as Lottie jumped down to sniff Colt's feet. "Don't be so sure about that. You're still her favorite."

Colt's sunny expression faltered. "No. I'm just a stand-in. Her favorite died not that long ago."

"I'm sorry."

He waved her off. "Don't be. We've all lost people." Colt bent down and scooped up the little dog. "Haven't we, Lottie?"

As he walked off, Madison leaned against her mom. "Do you think we'll be safe here?"

Her mom wrapped an arm back around Madison and squeezed. "We can hope."

DAY FORTY-SIX

CHAPTER TWENTY-NINE

DANI

CLIFTON COMPOUND
10:00 a.m.

DANI BLINKED HER WAY OUT OF A DREAM AND TURNED her head. The dirt and leaves and stink of animal were gone, replaced by soft lantern light and a blanket. She turned her head.

Colt sat beside her, head resting on his hand. He stared out at nothing. She opened her mouth to speak when his voice filled the silence.

"I know that you need to sleep, but if you could just wake up for a little while, I've got news."

She tried to say something, but he kept going.

"We've made it to the Cliftons' place and it's everything we could ask for. They've got a deep well and a garden and pigs and chickens. They've even rigged up a composting toilet." He snorted. "They're turning shit into fertilizer."

Dani smiled through the clearing fog.

"And the best part is that they've asked us to stay. We can have a life here, Dani. I know it's not what you wanted and we're back with strangers, but I think you'll like it here. God knows we need the break. We can't keep running. We need a chance to breathe." He pressed his fingers into his eyes. "But it would be great if you would wake up."

"Why is it we only get to sleep in a bed when someone almost dies?"

Colt spun around with a start. "You're awake!"

She nodded.

"For how long?"

"Long enough to know I'm not dead and stuck with you in the afterlife."

He grinned. "We made it."

"Is Larkin here?"

Colt nodded. "And Lottie, too."

Dani tried to sit up, but a wave of dizziness threw her back. "She's alive?"

"She's got a chewed-up ear and some scratches, but that dog's a trouper."

Dani closed her eyes in relief. "I thought the bear killed her."

"It almost killed you."

"That, too." So many thoughts and emotions swirled inside Dani's head. She managed to put voice to one of them. "Thanks for saving me. Again."

"Any time."

"How about we take a few days in between."

"I'd appreciate that." Colt leaned back in his chair and exhaled. "It'll be hard work living here. Everything they have they work hard to produce."

"Good. That means we'll have something to do."

"I've agreed to lead some raids into town to hunt for more supplies."

Dani swallowed. "I'll go, too."

"Not until you're one hundred percent."

"Fair enough." She chewed on her lip. "We can't screw this one up, Colt. These people can't die because of us."

"We won't. Not this time."

Dani nodded as the door to the room opened. A girl with blonde curls and a red bandana stuck her head inside. "Walter's about to broadcast. Didn't know if you wanted to listen."

"Thanks."

As the girl was about to leave, she caught sight of Dani. "You're awake."

Dani nodded.

"Welcome. It's good to have you."

The door shut behind her and Colt stood up. "That's Brianna. She's the daughter of the people who built this place."

"How old is she?"

"Twenty, I think. And there's two other kids about her age, too."

Dani didn't know what to say. She'd gotten so used to hanging out with Colt that seeing someone closer to her age never crossed her mind. Maybe staying there wouldn't be such a bad thing.

"Did she say Walter's broadcasting?"

Colt nodded. "He's got this crazy setup here with a ham radio and massive antennas. Said sometimes when they're listening they can pick up people across the country."

"No way."

"Want to listen?"

Dani nodded and let Colt help her off the cot. She wobbled, but managed to stand with his support. Together they hobbled out of the cabin and into an open area. She stopped to process it all.

Three cabins, a barn, pasture, and fruit trees. It was a mini working farm carved out of the forest. She couldn't believe it.

Colt helped her over to where Walter sat in front of an electronics setup fit for a radio station.

He smiled when he saw her. "Welcome back."

"Thanks."

"I can only broadcast for a couple minutes. It's too much of a drain on the solar." He turned back around and moved some dials and hit some buttons. "Good morning. The time is 10:30 a.m., Pacific Standard Time, and this is Walter Sloane.

Dani eased down to the ground with Colt's help and leaned against him while Walter spoke. She thought back to that night in the Wilkins family's basement and how they all gathered around the radio to listen to his broadcast.

She never thought she would be sitting behind the

same man, watching him as he spoke words of hope and encouragement to people all over. As she sat there, she caught sight of Lottie running through grass almost as tall as she was, her little pointed ears sticking up above the green.

Could they really be happy here? Could they really stay?

She turned to see two women side by side also listening. From the resemblance, Dani put it together: Walter's wife and daughter. Dani swallowed. This wouldn't be the same as Eugene. She wouldn't let it.

They would work together to survive out here, away from cities and towns and the threat of outsiders. She would contribute as much as she was able.

Walter cleared his throat as he wrapped up. "Every day you wake up is another day to celebrate. You're alive. You're breathing. Make the most of it. Take the opportunity you've been given and run with it. Even in the darkest moments hope still lingers like an unlit match. All it needs is a spark to light. Until next time, this is Walter Sloane. Good luck."

He clicked off the radio and his wife walked forward. She bent down and kissed the side of his head.

The daughter made her way over to Dani and crouched with an outstretched hand. "Hi. I'm Madison."

Dani took her hand and shook it. "Danielle, but everyone calls me Dani."

"Nice to meet you, Dani."

Lottie scampered up between them, yipping and twisting in circles. Both girls laughed.

"I think she likes it here."

"Seems that way." Colt reached out and helped her up to stand. "Now it's time you went back to bed."

Dani frowned, but didn't argue. Walking the handful of steps outside had tapped most of her strength. As they made it back inside, she turned to him. "Thanks for not giving up on me."

He took her by the shoulders. "I'll never quit on you, Dani. Never. We're in this together, no matter what happens next."

* * *

Thank you for reading book seven in the *After the EMP* series!

Looking for more *After the EMP*? You can find the rest of the series on Amazon.

If you haven't read *Darkness Falls*, the exclusive companion short story to the series, you can get it for free by subscribing to my newsletter:

www.harleytate.com/subscribe

If you were hundreds of miles from home when the world ended, how would you protect your family?

Walter started his day like any other by boarding a commercial jet, ready to fly the first leg of his international journey. Halfway to Seattle, he witnesses the unthinkable: the total loss of power as far as he can see.

Hundreds of miles from home, he'll do whatever it takes to get back to his wife and teenage daughter. Landing the plane is only the beginning.

* * *

ACKNOWLEDGMENTS

Thank you for reading *Hope Sparks*, book seven in the *After the EMP* saga. Now that Colt, Walter, and the rest of the group are finally together, they have a chance to heal, breathe, and start a new life.

These characters have been through so much in such a short period of time, but they have persevered through it all. I hope that if any one of us are ever faced with such challenges, that we too can rise up and find our hidden strength.

It seems every day the news brings brings more talk of potential threats, whether by nature or man. All we can do is prepare to the best of our ability and dig deep into our courage when the time comes. Thank you for coming with me on this fictional survival journey - it's been both a challenge and a joy to write!

Although I try to be as realistic as possible, I do take occasional liberties with regard to real places and things for the sake of the story. I hope you don't mind and can still go along for the ride!

If you enjoyed this book and have a moment, please consider leaving a review on Amazon. Every one helps new readers discover my work and helps me keep writing the stories you want to read.

I'm not sure what the new year will bring for either the cast of *After the EMP* or a new series I have in the works, but rest assured it will be full of new stories!

Until next time,

Harley

ABOUT HARLEY TATE

When the world as we know it falls apart, how far will you go to survive?

Harley Tate writes edge-of-your-seat post-apocalyptic fiction exploring what happens when ordinary people are faced with impossible choices.

Harley's first series, *After the EMP*, follows ordinary people attempting to survive in a world without power. When the nation's power grid is wrecked, it doesn't take long for society to fall apart. The end of life as we know it brings out the best and worst in all of us.

The apocalypse is only the beginning.

Contact Harley directly at:

www.harleytate.com
harley@harleytate.com

Made in the USA
Las Vegas, NV
12 September 2024